FORTUNE BOX

MADELEINE SWANN

ERASERHEAD PRESS
PORTLAND, OREGON

ERASERHEAD PRESS
P.O. BOX 10065
PORTLAND, OR 97296

www.eraserheadpress.com
facebook/eraserheadpress

ISBN: 978-1-62105-267-8
Copyright © 2018 by Madeleine Swann
Cover design copyright © 2018 by Eraserhead Press

Printed in the USA.

1

The first parcel arrived at a little flat in the centre of the city. Contrary to the postman's usual practice, when she didn't answer his ring on the buzzer, he was compelled to buzz someone else and climb the stairs to leave it at her front door.

They were lying to her. All the TV shows that told her to drink cocktails, to laugh at men's jokes, to look at them beneath her lashes, to go to places they'd be, to get a new hobby (one ancient magazine from the 50s suggested bee-keeping), to pretend not to think about meeting them altogether (while obviously thinking about meeting them) or otherwise be independent yet in charge yet vulnerable for them. She gave up reading magazines; they were too full of mixed signals and left her with a constant sense that she was doing it all wrong.

Now, as Meera sat opposite the man arguing with her about censorship in the coffee shop (good place for first meetings, neutral) she debated whether to throw coffee over him or just get up and leave. She imagined him screaming as his face melted. At least he'd stop gibbering about how filmmakers should think before making anything nasty. "You can't just ban a film for everyone because one arsehole decides to take it literally," she fumed. Was it normal to get this angry on a first meeting? She didn't care.

"What if someone sensitive sees it though?"

"That's not something everyone else should have to suffer for. Find out about it before you go see it." Earlier he had extolled the virtues of giving up modern life and forming a small village where 'someone baked the bread, and someone else chopped wood and so on.' He actually said it, despite it appearing in satires of hippies. It was the moment in which she knew there would not be a second meeting. That moment dropped on her head like a rock every time. Granted, it wasn't the world's biggest problem, but she didn't know how many more times she could go through it. That rock was painful.

"I'm really sorry," she looked at her watch. How long had they been sitting there? Uh-oh, only half an hour. Never mind, "I've got to get back to get some work done, I've left it to the last minute and my boss will be furious." In truth she'd finished that work yesterday, she couldn't even imagine leaving something this late.

"What a shame, OK," he went to kiss her on the cheek but she backed away, rushing out before the conversation about meeting again could take place.

On her walk home she was too sad to admire the beautiful city she'd moved to only two years ago. She felt like a cartoon character seeing couples and love related signs. Her hand gripped the phone in her pocket, but she decided against texting her friend. Instead she called the one number obligated to listen to her for all eternity, "Hi mum."

"Hello sweetheart. How's things?"

"Yeah. I dunno."

There was a soft sigh on the other end, "bad date?"

"Yeah. I'm sorry, you must be getting fed up of this."

"Of course not. Don't you think you're worrying a bit too much, though?" Meera pursed her lips and her mother rushed on, "I mean, you'll find someone. The more you worry, though, the more difficult it'll be. Just relax."

Meera knew she was right but she'd tried relaxing and even less had happened. Nobody talked to each other in bars anymore and there was certainly nobody attractive at work. "You're right, it's not exactly the world's biggest problem. I'm healthy, I'm young, everything's fine."

"Exactly," suddenly Meera's mum cackled like an 18th century bawd.

"Mum?"

"Sorry, it's your dad," she managed to say between gasps, "He's doing that face again, you know the one…" anything she said after that was indecipherable so Meera promised to call soon and rang off. She just wanted someone to go bowling with, to the pictures, a nice restaurant. Someone who thought she was a good person. She was supposed to be able to make herself happy and anything else was a bonus, but telling herself that had become exhausting. She'd always been so good at things at college, a perfectionist. She couldn't understand what had changed. Now she didn't even feel like she was good at her job. She pulled a weird face to exorcise the memory of typing up the wrong file and then breaking the photocopier, drawing a confused look from a passer-by.

"What the…" she picked up the plain cardboard box printed with Tower LTD Surprise Packages from outside her front door. That action made her feel like a proper grown-up at least. When she'd first moved in, after checking no-one else was around, she'd unlock her door, lock it and unlock it, sometimes five times in a row, just enjoying the sensation of having a door to herself.

Sitting in the rocking chair her mother insisted she take with her ("you always loved that chair, it calms your nerves, do it for your mother,") Meera slid the scissors down the edges of the cardboard and pulled it open: a packet of seeds and a tiny watering can. She examined the seed packet – nothing but a line drawing of a man in a superhero pose. With an ironic grin she pulled a china vase from the cupboard, hurried downstairs and filled it with earth from the scrap of a garden and trotted back up, a strange night before the holidays feeling buzzing in her chest. She tipped the single seed into the vase, splashed it with tap water and waited, chewing her nails and tapping her foot. Nothing.

She lay on the couch and flicked through the TV. She should have known it was stupid. What did she think would happen, a magical beanstalk would lead her up to a world of no work and happy times? She couldn't settle on a channel, instead vacantly flicking through repeats and things she hadn't wanted to see the first time around. "Hi!"

She screamed so loud it echoed from each corner of the room. The man now brushing dirt off held his hands up defensively, allowing his penis and balls to dangle freely, eyes wide with terror. Meera shut her mouth. The vase had tipped over and the earth was spilled over the table, and spots of it led to the naked man. It was impossible. Wasn't it? "Um, aren't you cold?"

He gave a half smile, "yeah, a bit." He was the kind of person she would pick out at a shop for men. He looked artistic, delicate, and handsome.

"There's a charity shop just down the road, I'll get you some clothes."

"Great, I'll make tea."

She had no idea of his size and grabbed anything vaguely fashionable. As she entered the main doors her neighbour, a middle aged fussy woman, stopped her, "did I hear screams coming from your room? Should I call the police? I knocked on your door but…"

"No, no, everything's fine, I dropped something," Meera darted upstairs, certain her visitor had evaporated.

He hadn't, he was sipping tea and flicking through an old magazine, as real and solid as the second hand chair he sat on. She could already see them ordering pasta in the fancy Italian she'd not been able to go to yet. She saw him laughing at her terrible bowling skills while she pretended to be annoyed, saw them sharing popcorn at the cinema (could seed people eat pasta or popcorn? This one had better). She pictured herself reading while he worked on something artistic, late night walks past teenage binge drinkers and tipsy women balancing on heels. They'd talk politics, films and art, and maybe she'd allow him a boob touch on the first night. Different rules apply to magical creatures, surely?

He gratefully took a red jumper and black trousers from her. "I actually think this one is better," she held up a blue shirt.

"This is fine."

"No, it...trust me this one's much nicer."

"I've almost got it on now," he said, though in truth only his arms were inside the itchy looking fabric.

"Please, just do it for me," Meera grabbed at the jumper. His eyes sharply met hers and Meera caught herself, reluctantly allowing him to finish dressing. It really was a horrible jumper. Something caught her eye, "what's that?"

Furrowing his brow, the Seed Man looked down at his chest, where green liquid poured liberally onto the carpet, "you broke my surface." He wobbled and caught hold of the table edge. Meera rushed to his side and led him to the sofa where she pulled up the offending item of clothing. His skin was soft as velvet and the liquid gushed from a small tear. She flapped her arms, hopping about like a frightened penguin.

"I'll get a bandage," she searched desperately through drawers in the kitchen and bathroom, finally locating some plasters her mum had been kind enough to force on her during the move. "I promise you'll be fine," she clumsily tore them from the packet and arranged them over the split, her fingers staining green under the torrent. He was worryingly pale.

Amazingly, it seemed to work. A little colour returned to his face and he sat up to sip some sweet tea. The happy scenes in Meera's head shone brightly once more like a cinema screen. "How do you feel? Up for a walk? You need some food."

"I...really?"

"Oh..." Meera sat back, aware of a faux pas. She should have kept quiet, allowed him to decide what their next move was. She couldn't quell a surge of impatience, she hadn't asked him to appear and now he couldn't do one thing she wanted? Immediately she felt like the world's biggest bitch, grateful he couldn't hear such horrible thoughts. "You lie back. I'll get us a takeaway. Pick a channel, here," she handed him the remote.

He lurched upright, "I'm fine, honestly. Let's go."

"No," she tugged gently on his arm, "I don't want

to go anymore, please sit down."

He sighed as though she were a thing that required great patience, "I'm fine. Let's go."

They made their way arm in arm through the huge Victorian shopping arcade, Meera pointing out to him her favourite parts such as the stained glass windows and period candle lamps. She told him she liked to pretend she was a Victorian lady buying luxuries for her Mansion. "That's sweet," he said, but the words were forced, as if he were saying it because he should.

"We can go back if you want."

"I'm fine," he snapped, irritation marring his features.

"Jeez, I was just concerned."

"Well, don't be, I'm fine, I thought we were having a nice time."

The Italian was busier and noisier than she expected, but it was fancy and clean and she felt special as the waiter showed them to their seat. A large pillar obstructed their view to the room length glass wall but a candle sputtered atop a bottle and romantic music seeped from the speakers nearby. Meera wondered if she should try holding Seed Man's hand or start a conversation, but when she looked up he was staring at the pillar, "that's kind of annoying."

"Not really, we can just look at each other."

"Of course," he smiled tightly, "you like this city, I can tell. What made you want to move here?"

This was more like it. They chatted happily until the waiter came and ordering went smoothly. Meera sipped her wine and a tiny speck of hope blossomed in her stomach. He really was handsome and they even shared a joke or two. He wasn't difficult, he was just passionate, and it was her fault things had got off to a shaky start, for goodness' sake. He was being gracious considering. Then dessert happened.

"Are you alright?" He was staring again at the pillar.

"I'm fine. It's just...I'm fine." He had a mouthful of chocolate brownie but didn't seem to taste it.

"What?"

"Well, what kind of place actually sits a table miles from the others, right by the kitchen doors and hidden from the outside world. Are they trying to tell us something? Are we the elephant couple?"

"OK," Meera reached for her bag, "I'm going home."

"No," Seed Man placed a hand on hers, "I'm sorry. I'm just in so much pain, it's making me moody."

Meera paused. He'd mentioned chest pain and now she couldn't go anywhere. She stared miserably down at his hand, the delicate fingers covering hers. She wished she liked what was attached to them more. "Are you sure you don't just want to go back? Maybe I should phone a hospital?"

"It's fine, really," he said. Meera never wanted to hear that sentence again, but he seemed genuine. The night could be salvaged, she was sure of it.

"OK."

The bowling alley and cinema were directly opposite one another. Meera, without thinking, headed for the bowling complex and Seed Man for the cinema. Meera's muscles tensed. Was she supposed to show she could be considerate, or put her foot down? It was so hard to tell. She was relieved when he placed an arm around her shoulder and guided her towards the bowling alley.

She should have known it was temporary. Before they arrived at the desk they should have known there wouldn't be games available immediately, they should have booked. She shouldn't have tried to start a conversation while they waited on the bench because she knew that his reply would be terse and irritated. She should have gone home and left him. No, she should be more understanding. She wasn't sure.

When the teenage boy told them they could have aisle 14 she stood up to follow him. Seed Man stayed put, "I'm not sure I'm in the mood, why don't we catch the film instead?"

"You can't go into a film when it's already been on for ten minutes."

"We'll pick it up."

"No. We...are...going...bowling." She grabbed his arm, ignoring his wince, certain he was over-reacting. She smiled politely at the boy, who recoiled in horror.

She typed in their names on the lane console and grabbed a ball, her rage sending it careening off to the side almost immediately. "Whoopsey," she shrieked, turning to Seed Man who watched in stunned silence from the seats, "your turn." He rose unsteadily, picking up a ball without checking its weight, his eyes on her as they passed each other as though watching a tiger for sudden movements. "Go, Seed Man!" Meera hopped up and down and clapped her hands, her frantic actions drawing whispers and glances. Seed Man swung his arms back and threw the ball, yelping like a trampled dog. "Well done," Meera screamed as the ball stopped halfway and curved geriatrically into the alley.

"I need help," Seed Man bent double.

"Don't be silly, you're really good."

"No, I really need help," green goo splashed onto the aisle. He turned to show her the river flowing from his chest, over his fingers, and down his legs. A small child screamed.

"Its fine," Meera seethed. An old lady had to be supported by her family before she collapsed to the ground, "it'll heal."

"Look at me," his face was twisted in primate fury, "Look what you did."

Meera strode towards him, grabbed his arm and pulled him out into the street, "we are going to have a romantic evening if I have to murder you to do it." Sensing the evaporation of her reason, Seed Man complied. She dragged him to a quiet, rural pathway lined with flowers that she had once pictured strolling through with a man she loved, putting her hand in his. "Don't those begonias smell beautiful," she breathed in deeply, "and those primroses, mmm..." her eyes flicked to his, "aren't they beautiful?" she growled.

"Yes, yes," tears speckled his eyes, "very lovely."

"Don't you want to buy me some?"

"Um..." her eyes hardened, "yes, I'd love to." The goo continued to pour and his breathing quickened as they made their way to the supermarket at the end of the path.

"Those are my favourites," she pointed at a bunch of Oriental lilies in the doorway and dug out a note from her pocket. Seed Man staggered towards them, whimpering again as a particularly large amount of goo sputtered over some roses. He clamped his free hand tighter over the wound to stem the flow, greeting the cashier wanly. She studied him suspiciously as she rang up the bouquet, almost forgetting to take any money.

"Keep the change," he said hoarsely.

"What?"

"Keep the...never mind." He took the change and returned to Meera's side. She held his hand once more and pulled him in the direction of the flat, stopping as they passed an ice cream shop.

"Oh, let's get some," she gushed, her cheeks feverishly red. "No, I'm watching my figure. Oh why not, it's a special occasion. I'll have vanilla."

Tears dripped from Seed Man's eyes as he leaned hard against the counter, "one vanilla cone please."

"You're not having one?"

He turned back to the shopkeeper, "and a cherry one please." His front was entirely saturated in green.

"Are you OK?" the shopkeeper's eyes darted from Seed Man to Meera and the phone behind the till.

"He's fine," Meera hissed.

"Fine," Seed Man whispered faintly. The shopkeeper hesitantly scooped the ice creams and handed them over, watching the pair leave with barely concealed horror.

"Tastes so good," Meera wolfed hers down and, seeing Seed Man's slow progress, ate his too. "Finished together," she giggled and laid her head against his chest, ignoring the green waterfall matting her hair. "I'm having such a nice time."

"Mm hmm."

They were back at her flats and Meera shyly took her key from her pocket, "I shouldn't ask you up, really, but I can trust you, I just know I can."

"But...you created me. This is technically where I live..."

"You're different, you're kind," she babbled, not seeming to hear him, "come on." He followed her up the stairs, bowing his head when a man on his way out did a double take. Green goo trailed along the carpet behind them. "This is my place," Meera unlocked the front door, closed it again and unlocked it, cackled loudly and ushered him in.

He fell with a thud to the floor, goo pooling around him. Meera knelt at his side, stroking his face, "we've got wine, beer, or Cherryade?"

"I think I'm dying."

"I'll get you some Cherryade."

She lifted his head to pour it down his throat, but he was unresponsive. "I like it too," she chuckled, not noticing it dribbling back out of his mouth and mixing with the green. "I don't want to seem forward but is it OK if I kiss you?" Seed Man grunted, his eyes unfocused. She lowered her lips to his, pressing them gently against his warm, soft mouth. The light had faded from his eyes when she sat back up. Perfect, it had been perfect.

2

The second parcel arrived at the pigeon hole of a room in student halls in a rural town far from the city. Cassandra had piled her purple and black hair on top of her head, and her facial piercings sparkled in the weak winter sun. A bedraggled purple feather boa spotted with dust was draped over her shoulders and her body was cinched into a black corset. She'd taken to practicing her dance for Tuesday night at the student bar in bare feet to avoid falling over, but the show was in two days and she still couldn't do it in heels. One of the other drab students passed her at the bottom of the stairs and she cheerily greeted them, not noticing their look of shock.

She squealed when she found the parcel, false nails pinging into the wall when she tore it open. "Humane traps?" she lifted the wire mesh box out and turned it over and over, but the answer was still missing. She texted her friend, Sally, "Hey, U Snd Jk Pressie? Wut?" She had to be behind this. She padded back up to her room, dangling it carelessly from one finger.

She yelped when a loud bang erupted from her door. It was Alicia, hands bunched at her sides, wearing a silly daisy print dress and not looking pleased. "Hi, Cassandra, can you turn your music down?" Cassandra did as she was told, though it had barely been above a murmur. Alicia had invited her over on their first day and, during their conversation, shown her the TV guide with the programmes she had wanted to watch circled. Cassandra, finding this hilarious, had told everyone on their floor and Alicia found out. Now, as well as inciting the girl's constant rage, Cassandra was haunted by a sense that she was a terrible person and vowed never to do anything like it again. As soon as Alicia left she turned the music back up.

Later that evening, everyone on their floor gathered in the kitchen for Sharon's birthday. Most sang the customary song sweetly, clasping carefully wrapped presents and cakes, except for Cassandra and Sally who had drunk too much vodka and screamed it at theme park volumes. The others eyed them disapprovingly and, as soon as the cake was cut, disappeared to the birthday girl's room and shut the door firmly against both of them. "Fine," said Sally, "we didn't want to come anyway."

They stumbled into Cassandra's room and poured themselves more vodka. "What's this?" Sally picked up the metal trap from her friend's chest of drawers.

"Dunno, some weirdo sent it. Watch my dance," she flung her clothes off in front of her friend and pulled on her corset, unable to secure it properly and leaving it half hanging off. She began the Lady Ga Ga song, stopping dead when she noticed Sally doubled over and laughing hysterically.

"What's wrong?" Sally stopped laughing.

"Nothing," Cassandra huffed, "gonna make a spliff."

Sally, aware she had offended her friend, tried to reassure her that her performance was funny in a way that was good, but Cassandra remained silently hunched over a rizla and bag of weed. After a few puffs she returned to herself, "I'm gonna pull out."

"You should do it."

"Dunno. Anyway, what's going on with you and Gavin?"

The night disappeared down a tunnel of alcohol and weed, until at 5 am the girls were staggering down the hall to the birthday girl's room, carrying the trap and trying to smother their giggles. "She'll probably trip over it and die," whispered Sally, laying it in front of her door. They snuck back and forgot the whole thing.

The next morning Cassandra woke to silence. It was unusual and gave her the sense she was missing out on something fun, so she pulled on some clothes and went to see where everyone had gone. The hallway was empty, the kitchen was empty, nobody chattered in any of the rooms. The only sound she heard was Sally's snores from her own room. She decided to knock for her friend when something sent her flying to the ground. "Oof," she grunted, rubbing her jaw. She sat up and searched for the offending item, screaming soundlessly when she saw every single girl from the kitchen party inside the tiny trap, staring up at her with miniscule eyes, begging in barely audible voices to be freed. "Fuck," Cassandra prodded the cage, sending them tumbling. "Oops, sorry." The girls screamed again. Cassandra picked them up and thumped on Sally's door, "Look at this shit."

"Holy...how the fuck did you do that?"

"It's not a trick, look!" Cassandra shook the cage slightly and the girls shrieked and wept in their mouse voices.

"We should let them out."

"No way. The show is tomorrow night. We'll take this onto the stage, and let them out, and they'll grow big again. Everyone will be amazed and like, how did you do that, and stuff."

"I dunno," Sally raised an eyebrow, "what if something happens to them?"

"It won't. We'll look after them. I'll leave a chocolate bar in there or something."

They hid the cage in Cassandra's drawer, discussing the big reveal, how it should be done and how grateful the girls would be once they were freed. Never again would they ask them to turn their music down or complain about weed smell. "We should go to the bar," Sally checked her watch, "we can plan better with drink."

Their friend James was playing pool with a boy Cassandra had always liked, and when they suggested continuing their game in town, the pair were all for it. Pints became shots, then smoking joints down the alley, then off to a club to drink more and take pills. The next day, the day of the performance, they awoke in Cassandra's bed. "Wake up," said Sally groggily, "Get the cage out."

Cassandra opened the drawer and wished she hadn't. She never wanted to open a drawer again. At the bottom of the cage was a single girl, Alicia, and she was surrounded by half eaten corpses. Even at her tiny size Cassandra could see the haunted expression in her eyes, the feral way her body shook, "we forgot to put the chocolate bar in. They must have really quick metabolisms or something."

"What do we do?"

"I don't know!"

"We...could...carry her down to the entrance and release her, without anyone knowing it was us?"

"OK," Cassandra felt she was destined to ruin Alicia's life. She would have done anything to take it back, to make it up to her. As it was, the mini-Alicia growled and flailed against the bars like a wild beast.

They snuck out, keeping their heads down to avoid seeing anyone. The entrance was a sign at the end of a long, rural road beside a security guard's office. They took a last look around and Cassandra pulled the cage from her coat, setting it on the ground. She pulled up the cage door and they dived for the bushes, crouching low. Alicia's manic screams were barely audible, but once past the cage she inflated back to her original size and the guard ran out to see what the commotion was, carrying his stick. Spying the girl, her arms flailing, eyes mad and bloody mouth gibbering, he called for police backup. Alicia tore down the path towards halls and the guard followed her, attempting to reason with the savage girl in the daisy print, blood stained dress, "It's OK, sweetheart, whatever it is we can talk about it."

She turned, eyed him wildly, and lunged, gripping him ferociously and tearing into his neck. Blood spurted over the grass and the guard bellowed, the sound clapping across the grounds. A police car screeched to a halt beside them and two officers leapt out, yelling at Alicia to get down. Alicia didn't pay any attention, simply carried on chewing merrily on windpipe. They jumped her, pinning her down. One cop radioed for an ambulance – amazingly the guard was still alive – while the other handcuffed Alicia while she tried to fling her off like a rodeo horse. The ambulance arrived and wrapped a tourniquet around the guard's throat while he made hideous gurgling sounds. "You're going to be OK," said the paramedic, "we'll get you to safety." Alicia's howls were the most ungodly, mind shattering sound Cassandra had ever heard, and the hairs rose over her body.

"Christ," said Sally as they watched the vehicles leave. Neither spoke for ten minutes in the heavy silence.

"What shall we do now?"

Sally shrugged, "smoke?"

"Smoke."

3

The third package arrived at a house share in the city.

Terry scuttled through the subway crowds like one of the mice, tiny and insignificant. Work had been worse than usual. Fed up with the boss not noticing him he'd built up the courage to suggest an idea, only to be given a pitying look. "Phil suggested the same thing only an hour ago," she said, "isn't that funny? Well done though." She had sounded like a nursery school teacher congratulating a child. Terry couldn't flee the scene quick enough, his bowels rumbling with embarrassment. Once he returned to his desk and saw his notes shining up at him the truth clicked – anyone walking past could have seen them, and someone had, Phil. Terry glared at Phil chatting away with his headset on, well on the path to working his way out of the call centre pool. Terry said nothing, of course, merely shoved his notepad back into his desk drawer and continued with his day. Now, with work behind him and nothing but an evening of internet browsing ahead, he kept his head down and hoped nobody gave him a hard time.

Stepping through his front door he noticed a parcel on the dining room table. Meant for one of his housemates probably. He set about making tea and glimpsed the name – his name. His housemate must have taken it in. Who would it be from? He didn't know anyone, and he'd never heard of Tower LTD or their surprise packages. He shook it, half expecting it to ominously tick. It was silent. He pulled clumsily at the edges before getting a knife, cutting his finger slightly before looking inside. A book with his face on the cover and a slip of paper beside it. Trembling, he flicked through the pages. It had to be Phil, or one of the other turds from his team. But how? Every personal thought, every intimate moment, was recorded in witty anecdotes. He flung it across the room. Horrible! How had they done this? He barely spoke to anyone let alone told them any of this.

After an hour he picked it up cautiously as though it might spontaneously combust. It really did make him sound interesting. If it weren't for the invasion of privacy he would be impressed. But it didn't make any sense. He barely even spoke to his own mother, he didn't keep a blog. His housemates only communicated to tell him to buy milk. How had this happened? He examined the slip of paper, "Get noticed? Sign." Bemused, he turned to the first page to see a big X beneath the title above his printed name. He couldn't. But what difference would it make? It was only signing a book.

He searched through the clutter on the kitchen table, locating a biro. He held it above the X for several seconds before taking the plunge...and nothing happened. He tucked it under his arm, not wanting his housemates to find it, and traipsed up the stairs. His bed was a mattress on the floor and the computer screen was its shining overlord. He added his coat to the many items of clothing on the single chair, changed into his pyjamas and typed the internet password. He fell back so quickly that the rest of his body didn't have time to catch him, causing him to hit his head against the wall. He sat up and looked again. Whoever was doing this had a lot of time on their hands.

My Life, And Other More Interesting Things was the subject of adverts, book blogs, normal blogs, Youtube videos, reviews and actual TV programmes. Terry ran to his housemate's room down the hall, "did you do this?"

"Do what?"

"The book, all of it."

"I haven't touched your precious book," the slovenly young man reached a hand down his pants and sniffed his fingers, "everyone knows about the signing tomorrow, I've already promised not to play online so you can get your precious sleep."

It had worked. Whatever effect signing the book had made, it worked. Terry couldn't stop smiling on his way back to his room.

A loud noise sliced through his sleep. Mumbling, Terry felt around for the source, locating his phone and trying to turn off the alarm. But it wasn't his alarm, it was his ringtone. Shit, was he late for work? "Hello?"

"Terry, where are you?"

"Just coming," he leapt from his bed and searched for his work clothes. They had gone. The clock said seven, he didn't have to be up for an hour. He thought back to the voice on the phone – female, smart, and unfamiliar, "who is this?"

A tut, "Dania. Wow, I knew you weren't a morning person but this is crazy."

"Sorry, yes, on my way." He paused, "where to?"

This time the moment of silence was filled with worry, "Hadley's, the book shop, remember?"

An hour later, Terry charged at the double doors of Hadley's only to clonk against the glass and stagger back. A figure appeared inside, her brow furrowed beneath a hijab. She gestured to him to try a side entrance and he followed her directions, finding an unassuming silver door. The shop was neat, its shelves promising comfort without clutter. Friendly posters claimed the importance of books and the different sections were clearly labelled. "Hi Terry," said the hijab woman, "this is Maria, she runs Hadley's." Terry recognised her voice as Dania.

"Hi," Maria's hand was shaking his before he had time to register her face.

"I'll get you a coffee or tea maybe?" said Dania.

"Tea, no sugar. Thanks," and she was gone.

Maria ran him through her clearly much loved shop and, somewhere distantly in his brain, Terry was moved, but all he really wanted to do was grab her by the shoulders and scream, "Who are you? And what am I doing here?" After several painfully long minutes she led him to a small table at the back of the room, groaning under a pile of the same book from the parcel – Terry's book, and all Terry's wriggly and uncomfortable secrets. His knees wobbled and he grabbed the edge of the table.

"Goodness, are you OK?"

"I'm fine I...it's just a bit," he swept his hand over the bizarre scene.

"It's a little overwhelming, I know," she guided him to the chair and sat him down like an Alzheimer's patient. He wanted to tell her it wasn't overwhelming, it was cheating, he didn't deserve this, but he smiled and nodded and answered the right things to the right questions. When Dania returned with a steaming cup Maria dashed to meet her and most likely explain that their author was a bit of a nutcase.

"Just relax," Dania smiled as she approached, using the same reassuring voice as Maria, "ask their name and be yourself."

The hordes trooped in around nine, lining up and politely waiting for a response before shyly muttering

'I loved your book' or 'can't wait for the next one,' and Terry smiled and nodded and signed and watched them go before the next one was in his face. If it was a joke, it was the most elaborate he had ever seen. There seemed to be hundreds of them chatting, laughing, filling the shop with excitement and joy, all because of him. His head crackled with something unfamiliar – pride.

The girl in front of him looked just like the others. Her hair was pulled back in a ponytail and she looked as if she had gotten up early especially for this. She smiled sweetly and placed the book in front of him, waited while he signed, nervously twitched for a half second before blurting, "I wanted to ask about chapter 14."

A metal pole of fear shot through him, "mmm -hmm?"

"It's just, that girl you liked, I'm not sure what she'd think if she knew you were following her around in the station, and following her into the staff room and stuff? Like, every day."

Sick threatened to explode from Terry's mouth. That was in there? His mind scrabbled for an appropriate response, "uh, I wanted to be honest, you know?"

"Oh, sure," she said unconvincingly, "it's just, I don't know if it was good idea, you know?"

Shame bugs crawled up the insides of Terry's skin. His anus contracted. He opened his mouth and hoped that what came out would salve the situation once and for all, "well, I'd best get on, there's lots of people here."

"Oh, OK, thanks," the girl politely moved aside and Terry exhaled all the nastiness. She was gone.

It was over. As he continued signing, however, he bristled. How dare the author, whoever they were, tell people about that? Last year was a horrible time. Beyond horrible. When he looked back all he could see was hideous black gloop, his life spent trying to swim through the hideous black gloop, and he'd relished anything that made him feel free of it, like her. Things had made sense to him that would horrify him now. His father had died, he was new to the city, he was alone, and she'd seemed...nice. He had turned up for work on that first day and she was the only one to say hello, ask if he was alright, if he wanted tea. In their break he'd waited for everyone to leave before asking for her number, the single most terrifying thing he'd ever done, and she'd been more than happy to give it.

Then things had changed. He knew he'd messaged too much, he knew he was doing it at the time, but he couldn't seem to stop. Each fresh message he sent would be the one to lead to something more, he was sure of it. This time she'd agree to go for a drink, this time she'd be as pleased to speak to him as he was her, but she stopped replying. It took a whole day to get the courage to actually call her up, only to find she'd changed her number. It destroyed him. He just wanted to be around her and soak up some of her happiness, and then he saw her at the station...

The queue dwindled and Terry slumped back in his seat. He hadn't realised how tense he was, muscles hurt that he didn't know he had. Dania congratulated him and offered him more tea which he declined, he just wanted to get home. "We've got an interview lined up with The Mix tomorrow, so get some rest and I'll pick you up at eight."

"Thanks for today, I enjoyed it."

"Definitely." Dania's mouth was tight and her eyes worried. Terry felt bad for her, she clearly worked far too hard.

Terry stretched out on his bed, enjoying the quiet. He'd always thought he wanted to be around people but forgot how noisy and stressful they were. He was slipping into sleep when his eyes snapped open. He couldn't relax before reading about himself one last time.

Excitedly he flicked the computer on, only to stare open mouthed at blogs, opinion pieces and tumblr posts, endless endless words, on the patriarchy. "Slice off his balls with a scalpel and make him eat them," screamed one, "Fuck white men and their tears," said another. Shaking, he clicked on the worst headline, 'Another CIS White Author Thinks Stalking Is Totally Fine.' It was followed by increasingly hostile accusations of perversion, rape and assault, but the bit that made Terry's head reel was a single tweet hanging centre-stage. His name was the handle and, for a split second, he assumed it was a fake set up by a troll, but the words used told him something else, 'I just wanted to be around her and soak up some of her happiness.' "That's not creepy at all," said the article, dripping with sarcasm.

"No," Terry covered his face with his hands, "no!"

He frantically searched his phone, locating Dania.

"I'm a little busy right now, why don't you..."

"Did you know about the tweet earlier?"

"Terry..."

"Did you?"

"It wasn't the smartest thing to say, I'll give you that. But we can work around it. These things can always be solved. We'll have a chat tomorrow before the interview, you'll address it with them and apologise and that'll be that."

"How do they know my thoughts?" He dug his fingers into his head, "how are they sharing them like this?"

"We can have someone at the agency take over your social media if you'd prefer?"

"Can they do that? Please, do that."

"Sure." The relief in Dania's voice was barely concealed and Terry resolved not to look online for the rest of the day, after looking at maybe two more articles. Four hours later he finally switched it off and curled into a ball, the tears drip dropping softly onto his blanket.

Dania made it sound so easy. She picked him up the next morning with a styrofoam cup of tea, chatting about inconsequential things like she hadn't just allowed a raging pervert into her car. It made Terry feel a little less bruised and battered.

They arrived at the café, joining a well-groomed woman who shook their hands and laid a dictaphone down on the table. Dania's words ran through his head like a mantra: relax, address the problem calmly, and everything will be fine. "Terry, what do you have to say to all those people who believe you're a stalker?"

Terry's knuckles cracked. He stared into this woman's cool blue eyes and wanted to push her off her chair. He wanted to see her fly back, her legs sticking up in the air while she flailed helplessly. He wanted to hit her, to keep hitting until there was nothing left. He did the next best thing, "Fuck them. I'm not a stalker, I have a right to say what I wanted. I don't deserve to be hushed up just because of who I am. So what, I'm a man, I'm white, what does that matter?"

"Of course," the woman eyes flashed ecstatically, "and what would you say to that girl you knew at work?"

"I thought we were friends but you chose to shut me out. I just wanted to meet people. I hope you're happy." His face twisted in a snarl. Releasing the rage was like picking off a scab, he knew it was wrong but it felt so good. "And don't think you can bother me now I'm famous," he added, "I have all the friends I need." This is all her fault, he raged inwardly.

"He's very busy today," said Dania, herding him from the café, "he really ought to get on." They sat in the car for several minutes, Dania opening her mouth to speak before closing it again. The euphoria was draining from Terry and his bed looked like a holy resort in his mind's eye. With a sigh Dania started the car, neither speaking a word until she dropped him off. "Bye, Terry," she said, "try to stay off the computer for a while."

Terry didn't stay off the computer. Another bolt of

horror tore through him when he read the latest blogs, almost every one calling for his death or some medieval punishment. He clicked on the top post and, hanging between the article like a rebel flag, was yet another tweet. Terry clicked to the timeline, bewildered to see a picture of himself he'd never taken and a bio he'd never written. Both were pretty routine, the photo looked like a studio shot and the bio was a simple list of writing credits (none of which he recognised). The tweets themselves were another story. The first today was a routine shout out that he was being interviewed, evidently by the agency, but the one after detailed his rage at the journalist and the third, the one that made Terry run for the toilet to vomit a boiling concoction, stated simply, 'To the girl at work: thought we were friends, you cold shouldered me. Don't think you can bother me now I'm famous.' Terry lay on the bathroom floor, knees drawn to his chest, sobbing so hard his kidneys could have fallen out.

After dark he emerged to find a missed call on his phone; Dania. Swallowing hard, he called her back. "Hi, Terry," she sounded chirpy. It was a good sign. "Just a sec," she sounded like she was getting up to find a quiet place, less of a good sign. "I've just been having a chat with Nadia and we've come to an agreement. We're very sorry but we're going to have to withdraw as your agents."

Her words were the final punch in a video game, "you are?"

"We can't work with someone who repeatedly goes

against our advice," she was struggling to stay cool, "I'm sorry again and best of luck."

Terry stared at the phone for a long time afterwards. His options had shrunk to whether to get a tequila or commit suicide. It was as though the entire world had yanked down his underwear, pointed and laughed. The text message was an even bigger shock. "Hey, buddy," it said, "heard about your troubles. We're here to help. Come into our office tomorrow at noon, we'll talk." Beneath was an address Terry vaguely recognised as a small side street near a coffee shop. Were they going to murder him? Or just beat him severely? He didn't sleep at all that night.

The day was cold and he wore his heavy coat with the hood pulled up. It doubled as a handy disguise, though when he stepped onto the street he was surprised by the lack of recognition in the public. Each step brought him closer to impending doom, yet to stay at home was to accept certain defeat and this at least was an opening. He checked his phone – Millar Street, here he was. His eyes darted about as he made his way down the alley but no-one was to be seen. He pressed the middle buzzer sharing its space with the café and another company at the top of the building, noting the chipped white paint and graffiti surrounding it. A voice crackled back and he was soon face to face with a young, skinny man in glasses. "Hey, I'm Simon," he said, "come up." Terry was led upstairs to a makeshift office. Trendy magazines graced a second hand table and Terry was invited to sit on one of two cracked leather sofas, "you're probably wondering who we are." The young man apparently wanted to savour his air of mystery.

"Yes."

"We're a brand new publishing house who isn't afraid to say the shit everyone else shies away from. We're not gonna take this shit anymore. Have you read those headlines about you?" Terry nodded, cheeks flushing with shame. "Fucked up," the guy nodded. "Why is it OK to call you names and threaten you because you're a white male. Oh, sorry," he put his fingers in quotations, "CIS. Can I get you anything? I just got some donuts, have one." As Terry chewed on the sugary dough, something released in his chest. He didn't know this man, but he seemed earnest and truly on his side, and he couldn't remember the last time someone had offered him food out of kindness. He coughed to choke back an onslaught of tears. "It's OK," the man took a seat beside him and patted his back. Terry was irretrievably, overtly weeping in front of a strange man. "We can't let them treat you like this. Come and join us, and we'll show 'em we can fight back."

Terry nodded weakly, "Ok."

"Cool. You should release a video, we'll record it right here, and you'll tell everyone you're not backing down, you've signed with us and..." his eyes were aflame, "you're going to write an even edgier, crazier book than before. You with me?"

"Yeah," his enthusiasm lit a spark in Terry, "let's do it."

"OK, just a sec," he handed Terry a tissue and went about setting up a fairly decent camera on a tripod. Talking had always filled Terry with dread ever since primary school when the teachers made classes stand up and talk about themselves. Before such exercises he often threw up and had to be sent home. The teachers even suggested a child psychologist to his mother. Now, though, staring down the lens, he told himself he wasn't the one talking, it was the publishing house and every disgruntled man accused of stalking. He took several breaths before forcing out the words, "Hi, I'm Terry Mcormack."

He'd heard of words sticking in throats before, but these wouldn't even reach his stomach. He swallowed, trying to ignore the bead of sweat piercing his forehead. He clenched, forcing speech up his body, "and I've noticed something toxic about our community lately…"

He remained in the office that afternoon, checking and rechecking the responses, both written and spoken. Headlines shrieked of the "controversial author" who "slammed women complaining of problematic content." His video was the most shared of that year so far, but the comments were horrific. Terry's bowels contracted. His rage had subsided once more and all that remained was fear and regret.

"Relax," the young man embraced him and Terry, not wanting to be rude, allowed him. "This is good, the message is spreading."

Terry couldn't look at a person when expressing

negativity. He focused on his threadbare shoelaces, "that wasn't what I was trying to say. I didn't mean to," he waved his hands, "have a go at all women. I just wanted people who were reading stuff that wasn't there into my work to stop…doing that." He sighed, knowing how stupid he sounded.

"Right," Simon placed a hand on Terry's shoulder, "you just want to write what comes from your gut, but they won't let you. Everything's…" his lip curled in revulsion, "problematic." Terry felt as though he'd been thrown into a swimming pool filled with something he didn't understand. He almost missed the black goo. At least it was familiar. Was Simon's point the same as the one he was trying to make? What was his point? "We got you, man," said Simon and, with those words, Terry gave in. His entire body relaxed. He'd never been 'got' before. It felt good. He'd found a life raft. "There's no time to rest on your laurels, though," said Simon, pouring Terry a beer from a miniature fridge, "We've got to go further, push harder."

"We do?"

"Sure. You're all over the internet right now but what do you think is gonna happen tomorrow?" Terry pretended he was about to answer, not confident enough to actually speak, "that's right, they'll forget you. We can't let that happen. So, we're gonna make another video and, first sign of a lull, up it goes. Then you're gonna go home and write another book and, this time, don't leave anything out. No pandering, no fear.

Fuck those SJWs and their snowflake whining," his face reddened with primate rage.

Terry's hands slid apart from the sudden torrent of sweat. The camera was on and staring right into the dark back alleys of his mind. He clenched his fists and sat straight, "I spoke a little about those people who like finding fault and censoring artists, but it goes further. Much further, and something has to be done."

Terry nodded at yet another passerby who recognised him in the tube station. He checked his twitter account, which made so much noise lately he could only turn it on for a few minutes at a time. Most of it was death threats, which still shook him, but he was learning to cope. It wasn't technically aimed at him; it was his alter ego, a mythical figure, the Robin Hood of truth. He didn't really need to look at all, he thought the words and they appeared in his timeline. It was only grim curiosity that lured him when he was alone. He turned off the app, pocketed his hand and secretly pinched his thigh. He wanted, needed, to stop thinking about it. His new book was taking care of itself and now he was on his way to meet a much larger publishing house. He'd make sure Simon was well looked after, obviously, but he couldn't turn down an opportunity to grow.

The station was packed and people barely noticed the faces of those around them, except if they were in the way of a sign. If they had they would have seen a young man with straight shoulders, hands in pockets and a permanent, fixed upturn at the corners of his mouth, and perhaps even recognised him. He passed a newsagent, deciding to buy a magazine, when a familiar figure at the stand caught his eye. She'd come to represent so much unfairness in his life that it was a shock to see her as an average person. He was immediately sucked back into his younger, insecure body. Perhaps he should just stroll over and start a conversation. Enough time had passed, he was a different man now, and maybe they could bury the hatchet. Maybe she'd even be impressed, been harbouring a secret desire but hadn't been able to act on it for one reason or another.

When she met his eyes her face turned from blank, to confused recognition, to burning humiliation and rage. She seemed to decide whether to speak, instead turning her head in dismissal. Terry opened his mouth uselessly but stopped. There was nothing he could say against such a reaction. Furious, he left without buying.

The fourth parcel arrived at a small flat in the city. Inside was a small, blue glass bottle with a tag attached in string, and written on that tag was the word 'Lies.' Next to it was a freshly baked mini muffin covered in rainbow sprinkles, and written on the muffin in sugar icing was the word 'Truth.' Katya stared at them for a long time. She knew a sane person wouldn't consume anything sent through the post, but also felt an overwhelming and unexplainable urge to choose one. "I never lie," she thought to herself, "and that muffin looks amazing. So…down the hatch!"

The toilet of the community college wasn't the best place to have a meltdown, physical or otherwise. The main door would squeak open every ten minutes or so and footsteps thundered to the only other cubicle or, worse, wait close by for her or the other occupant to finish. Katya checked her watch; she had ten minutes till the start of her first lesson and she still didn't know where to go. "Stop it," she hissed at the wet rash growing on her arm. The red mucus appeared on her wrist after eating the muffin and now wept down to her elbow. She'd just have to pull her sleeve down and hope blood didn't get on her nice new blouse. She had to make this class work, there was nothing left.

She swept into the classroom. She was a strong woman without baggage and there was no itchy red mark on her body. The other students looked up from a set of three tables pushed together, their bland faces barely containing features. One girl in peach looked like a T Shirt washed too many times. Another was a young man she wouldn't look twice at in a club. The last was an overweight woman with a blinking problem. Katya couldn't believe she had been so worried, she was definitely the most interesting person in the room.

"Hello everyone," she sat gracefully at the end of the table, making sure they caught a glimpse of her curves in the dress she had made. They seemed nice enough, and as they chatted about their husbands or jobs or friends they expanded from two dimensional cut-outs to real people. Katya scratched her elbow, trying to hide her wince when she caught an open sore. "Oh, I've lived all over," she said, "I did fashion at Saint Martin's and sell clothes on my website."

"Goodness," the overweight lady blinked, "what do

you need basic business studies for?"

"Oh," Katya smiled, "it doesn't hurt to improve your skills." Her elbow burned.

The teacher, a woman with a grey bowl haircut and sharp suit, arrived late apologizing profusely. The rest of the day was spent introducing themselves to each other and covering the year's modules on a white board. Katya sparkled with excitement, this was taking her a thousand steps towards her goal. She was getting back on track. Her website would be up and running, followed by her business, and no more dead end jobs. Reality was finally catching up.

She waved goodbye to the others at the end of the day. She was a good person, she could look beyond their boring exteriors and see what was inside. They'd enjoyed her fashion stories and she had enjoyed sharing them.

Her flat was dark and quiet. It was always dark and quiet. As soon as she shut the front door she yanked up her sleeve, only to find the rash had worked itself to her torso. She scratched and scratched as though fleas nipped her skin, stripping off her clothes and tearlessly sobbing when she saw her entire body was covered. The hospital, she had to call the hospital. No, the out of hours doctor, that's what she'd try first.

Her finger dialed the first 1 before something sickening caught her eye - the rash on her leg was strange, as though something nestled beneath. She prodded the long, thin red mark striping her thigh and recoiled when she felt several, golf ball sized objects. She placed the handset back. No one could know. It was too disgusting. The thought of anyone seeing them was…impossible.

Shakily she switched on the TV and all the lights and everything was better. Her front room was small but tastefully decorated and it was easy to forget anything was wrong at all. Her hands clawed, she had to stop her scratching fingers. In front of the TV an easel held a medium sized canvas of a half painted Kim Kardashian portrait. She sat on the stool and observed the work she had done the night before. It was a little embarrassing but nobody would see, so who cared? She had tried painting Naomi Campbell or Alexander McQueen but her interest always waned, so the Kardashians it was. She picked up the paintbrush. This was good. A little creativity was all she needed. Soon she would be creative all day every day AND get paid for it.

The phone rang and she yelped, calming a little when she heard her mother's voice, at least temporarily. "Yes, sold quite a few, got a lot of sewing to do tonight." Katya stared down at her toes, waiting for the polite moment to say goodbye. It was just easier not to speak about how she was doing.

"Oh I'm so pleased. Is Mike being supportive?"

"Yeah, he's here right now."

"Is he? Tell him not to distract you too much."

"I will," Katya laughed, "Mum says don't distract me," she said to the empty chair. She imagined the scene from her mum's perspective and took comfort.

"You will come and see us soon, won't you?" Katya

promised she would, knowing full well she couldn't. Why did she keep asking? It was exhausting. An afternoon with both of them asking after Mike and her business was all she needed. She thought of an afternoon curled up beside her mother on the sofa and felt a familiar pang, so she hurriedly said goodbye and returned to the stool. Her painting didn't seem as good as it had. In her memory it had been an almost perfect rendition yet the face staring back now appeared wonky. Did it look more like Jim Morrison? Katya picked up her brush and threw it to the floor, savouring the flash of rage, welcoming it. It burned from her core. Her rash now screamed for attention and she scratched hard, still staring at the hateful painting. She hissed inwardly when her nail caught tender flesh and she supposed she ought to check the damage, but couldn't bring herself to do it. No, she had to. Her stomach rolled: a large gash now ran down her belly and one of the golf ball things threatened to burst free. She gently pulled her skin apart but still the thing wasn't quite visible. She swallowed vomit and picked the paintbrush back up, it wasn't as bad as she was making out, it was a really good likeness. She was just having a doubting moment.

The next morning she flounced into the lesson, booming an extravagant hello. She swallowed hard to dispel her dry mouth and calm her heart, taking a seat with the grace of a swan. "Hi," said the others, admiring her fancy appearance.

"Morning," chirped the teacher as she bustled in,

"today we'll have a look at the basics of branding. Katya, why don't you tell us a little about your fashion website?" Katya smiled but no words emerged. Her thoughts Catherine wheeled. "You know, did you hire a web designer, did you do it, what's the overall theme and look?"

After opening and closing her mouth a few times Katya forced out her voice, "it's...chic," all eyes were on her, "it's elegant, with...clean lines," she was warming up and moving her hands more, "I hired a designer to do it but I told him what to do."

"Is it the same as the clothes you do?" asked the blinky lady, "you could make us outfits for interviews." They laughed but the hope was real.

"Oh, absolutely," Katya puffed up, "when I've got time. I mean, I've got mannequins all over the place with half-finished outfits on all of them. If only my flat was as neat as my website."

"Can we see it?" asked washed out girl, Emily.

Katya's hands shook, "It's under construction at the moment. I can show you next week, it'll be back up next week."

"Not a problem," said the teacher, sensing a dangerous moment, "let's move on."

After the lesson Katya tried to scurry from the classroom before conversation was initiated, but blinky lady – Eileen – was already calling her, "we're going to the Bell later, did you want to join us?"

"I probably shouldn't, I've got quite a bit of sewing to do."

"Oh go on," said the young man, Samar, "have an evening off, go wild."

"OK, but, would you mind meeting me at the shop near me? I've got to get a couple of bits and...it'd be easier if you met me there instead of mine."

"OK," said Eileen, and Katya hurried away.

Katya slammed the front door. Her body burned and she flung her hands this way and that, scratching deep inside, her fingers prodding beneath the skin's surface. She stripped to allow her nails more access but stopped. Hundreds of golf balls now pressed against the many gashes and one on her wrist, where it had all begun, was almost protruding. She swallowed a scream - from within the wound a pupil surrounded by a blue iris dilated, as if it could see her. Frantically she checked the rest of her, finding another almost poking from her thigh, this one brown. She whimpered but still they stared dispassionately back, following her face whichever direction she moved. She staggered to the toilet and vomited a boiling concoction of fear and the day's lunch before curling into a ball on the cold tiles.

Hours passed. Should she call someone? Who should that be? Suddenly it was five minutes past seven and she remembered the night's meeting. She couldn't go. She had to go, no-one must know how disgusting she was. Wishing she'd taken Eileen's number she pulled on her dress and tights and burst through the door, expecting them to be waiting up the road. She was so surprised to see her face through the window of Eileen's little Ford as she drove past that she stumbled and fell, landing hard on her knee. Something popped, don't think about it, don't think about it. Eileen parked up and rushed to her side before she could close her front door and the woman's face as she took in the lack of mannequins and dress making paraphernalia was like a bucket of cold slime over Katya. "I tidied up at last," she said weakly.

"Oh, well done," Eileen's smile was fixed, "always nice to have a spring clean."

In the pub, each time Katya turned, the others whispered and when she returned from the toilet they stopped talking suspiciously fast. "We were just saying how nervous we all are of the exam," said Eileen.

"God knows I still don't understand half of it even after revising," grinned Samar. It was perfectly obvious it hadn't been the subject of their conversation.

"Still," said Emily, "you should be alright, Katya. You've been doing this sort of thing for ages." Katya didn't like the look in the girl's eyes or the curl on her lip. She shouldn't say anything. She should brush it off.

"What do you mean by that?"

"Ah," Emily's mouth opened in shock.

"She just meant that you should do well," Eileen said, her eyebrows raised. Katya tried to speak but couldn't.

"Um, I think I'm gonna be off," said Samar, "we've got quite a lot to do tomorrow."

Once he was gone Katya stood abruptly, "I'd best be off too." She waved a cheery goodbye and retreated.

Once inside she collapsed on the sofa. She couldn't remove her dress. The thought of seeing the eyes again was too much. She felt them, though, as they swivelled and searched for her, making moist glooping noises. She put her hands over her ears and screwed up her face against any tears threatening to escape.

The next morning. This was it, she knew what she had to do. She arrived in the classroom determined, "Hello all." Their greeting seemed cheerful but something was missing, and Katya knew how to fix it. "So I've been thinking about everyone's interview outfits," did Emily just hide a smirk? "I'd like to make a really colorful dress for you, Emily, and something more reserved for you two?" Their nods and quiet agreements weren't quite the enthusiastic responses she'd hoped for, but it was something so she charged on. Her college housemate had taught her to make a few thing before she'd dropped out, it wasn't hard, she could do this. "Come with me," she headed for the exit.

"Um," said Samar and Emily.

"Class will start any minute," said Eileen.

"It won't take long," Katya's tone verged on pleading. Did they notice? No, she'd got away with it. They followed her into the fashion room filled with fabric and mannequins at the end of the hall, dragging their reluctance behind them. "Eileen, why don't you let me fit it for you?"

"I'd rather not," Eileen glanced at the door.

"Right," Katya laughed, "Emily?"

"Why don't you show us what it looks like on you?" Samar and Eileen shot Emily a look Katya didn't quite understand. Every muscle in her body contracted, "OK. It's exciting, isn't it?" She organized them into seats by the wall and trotted to the changing stand, carrying a roll of bright orange cloth and pins. She watched herself pull material free and wrap it around her body in a bulging, wrinkly mess in the mirror on the wall. Holding it in place with one hand she straightened her top underneath, but she still looked pregnant. She couldn't do what she was thinking, could she? She had no choice if she didn't want to look ridiculous. She threw the cloth aside and removed her clothes, studiously avoiding the mirror. Each time she thought she had successfully pinned it together a piece fell away, exposing things she couldn't bear to see. So she carried on, wrapping and wrapping, until finally she was mummified, but in a completely fabulous, clearly talented way. She stuck in enough pins to hold it and tried not to breathe in the moldy attic smell from the stand. Or…was it from something else? No, of course not.

"We really ought to go," Eileen called.

"Finished," she emerged, sashaying with as much attitude as she could muster towards them, "What do you think? This color would really compliment Emily's complexion, and..." She never got to finish her sentence. The first pin gave way, causing the fabric to slide downwards and yank out the rest. Her safety net crumpled to the floor and Katya stood in the middle of the room, naked, three pairs of eyes staring at her and a thousand staring back at them. Barely a patch of free skin was left, her body a terrain of blinking newborns to large, encrusted bloaters. The ones around her thighs were the worst, red raw and dripping with filmy liquid. Samar vomited and the other two screamed, and Katya tried desperately to cover herself, but it was too late. She had been seen, there was nowhere left to hide, the truth was out.

5

The fifth package arrived at 37 Leafy Villas, in the cul-de-sac of a small village. The bell tinkled delightfully when the postman rang it, but the woman who answered didn't match up. With her short, fluffy hair springing in all directions and long face red with frustration, she looked to him like a bull about to charge. "Thank you," Millicent barked, slamming the door.

She chucked it down and returned to the source of today's disaster, a broken boiler. Winter was checking its watch and her boiler had decided to break. Her fingers reached for the phone and pulled back for the fifth time that day. She knew what he'd say, "you're the one who deals with the house things, I go to work. Help me out a little, I can't do everything." Inhaling sharply, she snatched up the receiver.

"Mr Heather's office, can I help?"

"Is Giles back yet?"

"I'm afraid not Mrs Heather, can I take a message?"

Millicent sighed, "No. Just tell him to call home."

"Of course Mrs Heather," but Millicent was already slamming the phone down. She paced the front room. If the boiler wasn't working, Giles would have even less reason to come home. She caught a glimpse of herself in the mirror, her big body mocking her. She used to be slim and pretty and Giles had liked to show her off, but now he was always making excuses to stay away. She barged into the airing cupboard and kicked the pipes.

"Why are you such a cunt?" The naughtiness of the word fizzed in her blood and she felt quite good afterwards, wondering if Mary next door had heard. She could already see the look of shock on the woman's face when they next ran into each other. Would she still stop to talk about their latest gadget or car they'd bought last week, or would the sound of Millicent screeching 'cunt' through the walls come back to haunt her?

As good as the feeling was it didn't last. She supposed she ought to phone the plumber. God, how she hated talking on the phone. Interaction in general was enough to make her stomach bubble like a witch's cauldron. She hadn't always been that way – sun-filled memories of working in an office came back to her. When had it changed? Not immediately after her marriage, but not long after. A slow fizzle out of social interaction until not even friends remained because it was easier than explaining why her husband was so... not rude. Never rude. He just had a certain way of looking through people as if they weren't there, of letting them know they had no meaning in his life. She knew her friends might be able to explain it away when he did it to them, though it was still embarrassing, but she couldn't deal with the look in their eyes when he did it to his own wife.

Something caught her eye – the package. It was the perfect way to postpone the inevitable. She tore into it, relishing the destructive act, falling back when a suited man dived out and forward rolled like an action movie star to the bottom of the stairs. "Who are you?"

"Good day," he stood, smoothing his suit and holding out his hand, "I'm Dr Melford."

"Millicent. Wait," she put a hand to her forehead, wondering if she'd perhaps run a temperature, "what are you doing in my house?"

"I've come to fix the boiler."

She gawped at him, this strange little man with smooth black hair parted neatly in the middle, standing in front of her as if he hadn't just leapt from a box, "right."

"Why don't I go on up and have a look at the damage?" he started up the stairs and Millicent opened the biscuit tin. Everything was better with biscuits. No, she placed the tin back on the table. She had to lose weight, and not just for Giles. No biscuits.

"Do you want a cup of tea?" she called up. He muttered something. Must be on the phone. She tried again, "tea?"

"We're fine thanks."

We? Things were not normal. That man had sprung from a box and it was definitely not the sort of thing other people took in their stride. Millicent tried to sneak upstairs unnoticed but a creaky step betrayed her. The man was sitting on the dressing room stool in the hallway facing the open door of the airing cupboard. "Ah," he said, a polite but firm expression on his face, "I'm afraid this is the private section of the therapy. We can ask you to join us in a moment if," he turned to the boiler, "that's alright with you?" A second of silence followed. "Quite," the man – therapist? – chuckled softly. "So if you wouldn't mind?" he held a hand up to the stairs indicating that she should go back down them. Millicent opened her mouth to speak but found herself complying, sitting once more on the floral armchair in the front room. She hated this furniture but it seemed to be the right stuff for the neighbourhood. It was the sort of thing everybody else had. In fact, she looked about their substantial home with its sturdy upholstery and mint green carpet, everything they owned was here because it was the right sort of thing. She thought back to a time when she and Giles had made a purchase because they loved it but it was too long ago to remember what it was.

"We're ready for you now," the therapist called. Millicent had almost forgotten he was there and trudged back up, taking a seat on the little stepping stool he had placed beside his own.

"How much will it be?"

"How much do you value peace of mind?" He spoke in infuriatingly soothing tones.

"It depends how much it costs."

"Ah," he softly chuckled again, "money." Millicent wanted to twat him with the stool. "It won't cost you money, merely your time."

Millicent felt her entire body retreat to the edge of the stool so she could take in more of him, as if by studying him she could work out what gobbledygook he was speaking, "no money? What, free?"

"Is anything ever free?" He sighed, and her fingers again twitched with violent longing. He straightened in his seat and clapped his hands, "let's begin shall we? Boiler here says he feels ignored."

Millicent snorted, then realised he was serious. "What are we supposed to do to include it? Play cards with it?"

"Why don't you start by sharing your feelings?"

She stood, "OK, it's got silly now. You've had your fun."

"Don't you want this fixed by the time Giles comes home," he seemed pleased with himself, "if he actually does come home." She sat with a plop. Her buttocks slapped together and made a cracking sound, as if to emphasise her sad life. She hated the boiler, and hated this man, and hated Giles, but mostly she hated herself. "Now," he gestured from her to the boiler.

"I didn't realise I was supposed to make you feel included," she shrugged. The therapist urged her on and she racked her brain for more to say, "I suppose I'll make more of an effort in future." Silence.

"What do you make of his reply?" the therapist asked her earnestly.

"There wasn't one." Millicent's head prickled the way it had when a school teacher had asked her a question.

The therapist turned back to the boiler and nodded his head several times, attempted to speak, then paused, apparently cut off. He turned to Millicent, "he felt very dismissed by your comment."

"I'm not sure what it really expected," Millicent's mind melted down a long and winding plug hole. She waved goodbye to it and all things sane. The therapist clasped his hands, seemingly struggling with how to get his point across. Millicent had an ugly flashback to the way Giles would smile patiently at her complaints before dismissing them, even when they had made perfect sense during the day. By the time she was face to face with him they sounded less and less reasonable. "Why don't I come to London with you this weekend?" she would say, or "why don't we paint the house together?" She suggested things less and less, until finally she did things without asking to avoid being told no or feeling rejected. Now, in the hallway talking to a boiler, all her rage spilled from her mouth. "You've got it easy. Why do you get to be the one who decides you've had enough? Why don't I? I've just got to keep going and going, doing what's expected."

"Good, good," the therapist nodded emphatically. Millicent huffed. This was ridiculous. It was time to throw him out now. Then she heard it, a deep, radio voice with perfect diction and swoon inducing bass.

"Maybe I didn't have a choice," it said. Millicent

blinked, got up to touch the pipes, then the boiler itself.

"You what?"

"Please don't do that. I said maybe I didn't have a choice."

"You spoke." Dumbfounded, she staggered back to her seat. The therapist helped her down, evidently worried she might pass out.

"We've established that," the boiler sulked.

"Now," the therapist said, "let's keep things civil. We need to maintain an open and constructive dialogue."

"You spoke," said Millicent again.

"Boiler," the therapist attempted to steer things back on track, "how do you think Millicent has been coping lately?"

There was an intake of breath, and the response was considered, "not well. Her husband is a douche."

"He is not," Millicent fumed, "how dare you."

"Alright, alright," the therapist's hands were up in defence, "let's please refrain from abusive language."

"Fine," said the boiler, "he's an unpleasant man."

"He is..." Millicent stopped short. She couldn't finish her sentence because the boiler was right. Giles was a douche.

"See, you agree."

"How does that make you feel?" asked the therapist.

"The boiler is very rude," she folded her arms, "Giles is very tired from work, and it makes him a bit distant I suppose. We did used to talk and...we don't as much. It's this client, he's horribly awkward and Giles gets so cross that he has to spend so much time with them and..." the truth cracked through her brain. She wished it hadn't, she was happier before the crack, but it was there now and she couldn't help but know. "He's having an affair."

"Well, duh."

"Now, now," the therapist said, "Millicent needs our support, not sarcasm. How do you think you'd feel in this situation?"

"I wouldn't have an affair."

"Yes you would," Millicent's shoulders slumped, "anyone would. I'm a huge fat stupid fucking dumpling." She burst into noisy tears, snot running down her top lip. The therapist tapped her shoulder in awkward comfort and handed her a tissue. She blew her nose. Several minutes passed in which nobody spoke. Then, feeling oddly better, Millicent sighed. "I wanted children, but Giles didn't. It's probably a good thing, they wouldn't have to see all this."

"I really wouldn't have an affair," said the radio voice.

Millicent sniffed back a glob of snot, "really?"

"No."

"How does that make you feel?" said the therapist, and Millicent was vaguely aware that he had left his seat and was backing towards the top of the stairs.

"Good, I suppose. Why wouldn't you have an affair?"

"You're pretty, and funny, and you can go outside. You can tell me about all the things that happen outside the airing cupboard."

Millicent blushed, feeling like a woman in the

black and white romance films she loved so much, "you think I'm funny?"

"Definitely, he never appreciated you. He barely even listens to you."

Millicent's shoulders bunched again, "I know. I'm just the embarrassment indoors."

"How long has it been since you even kissed?"

"Oh, God, ages. Weeks. Months!"

"I...always wanted to kiss you." Millicent's head jerked up. Surely it was having a joke. Why would the boiler, with his sophisticated voice and fancy pipes, ever want to kiss her? "Why don't you kiss me now?"

Millicent's hands flew to her cheeks. They were burning. She turned to the therapist, expecting him to tell her such things would never be allowed, but he was nodding his encouragement. Doubting herself and convinced the pair would just laugh at her afterwards, she made her way to the object of tiny dials and white surfaces. She puckered her lips, not wanting the moment to be over, and pressed them against it's cool surface.

The house ticked into life. Heat flowed through the pipes and the radiators creaked into action. The heat of Millicent's kiss burned throughout the house. "Wonderful," the therapist clapped his hands, "we're back in action. See, that wasn't so hard." Millicent smiled, sadness in her belly. Was that all the kiss was for?

A key turned in the door. Giles! "What am I supposed to tell him?" she hissed.

"What do you think you should tell him?" said the

therapist. Millicent flapped. She turned to the boiler. What did the boiler want? It was frustratingly silent.

"Millicent," roared Giles, "why's it so bloody cold in here?"

"Coming," said Millicent, hating her placating tone. She hurried down the steps to face a predictably stern faced Giles. In that moment she realised she hated him, his bushy eyebrows and stupid high standards, which seemed to apply to no-one but her.

"Been busy today again I see," his lip curled in an ironic grin at her dishevelled appearance. That moment changed everything for Millicent.

"Actually, I have. I fixed the boiler." Before he could comment she rushed on, "and I don't need you anymore."

His mouth opened in shock, "I beg your pardon?"

"I know all about your fancy lady and you are no longer welcome here."

"I'm sorry, but have you gone quite mad?"

"No," said Millicent, hands on hips, "I haven't."

"OK," Giles raised a nervous hand as if fending off a tiger, "whatever she said it's nonsense. She's this woman Terrence and I met at the Con club, she's taken a liking to me and…"

"The boiler and I are in love and we want you to move out right now."

"The…what on earth are you talking about? Oh God, you've gone funny."

"Get out!" Millicent shooed him, "out!"

"This isn't amusing," he wailed as he was pushed out the front door, "I understand, you're upset, but she's honestly just a mad woman, nothing happened…" but Millicent didn't hear him. She bolted it shut and vowed to have the locks changed in the morning. He'd probably try to evict her but she wasn't too low to stoop to blackmail.

She checked the boiler for signs of life, despair threatening to burst from her chest. The therapist had disappeared and it seemed her new love had too. "Hello?" she tapped it gently. Nothing. She sank onto the stool and sobbed quietly. What had she done? What would Giles tell everybody?

"Well done," said a radio voice, "you should have kicked him in the backside."

"Boiler!" she squealed. She flung her hands around its smooth contours, and when they kissed it was as hot as a summer's day.

6

The sixth parcel arrived at a pleasant enough semi-detached house not too far from the city centre. A small pile of items waiting to be sold sat by the front door, including a beautifully carved but awkwardly sized cabinet almost reaching Mark's chest. Someone had wanted to buy it on Ebay last week but didn't turn up, so there it remained surrounded by cushions and cutlery.

When the doorbell rang, Mark accepted the package from the postman with a false air of nonchalance, as if he always received exciting packages. The postman smiled politely and had already forgotten him by the time he was at the next house. Mark sat on the sofa, excited and nervous, wondering if Karina had gotten him a surprise to celebrate their move. He tore at the cardboard, annoyed at the amount of sellotape, eventually arriving at the good stuff inside. "What the fuck?" his excitement collapsed. At the bottom of the package was a slip of paper containing a small drawing of a cabinet – the exact cabinet by Mark's front door. Beneath it was a scribbled map, a child's stick drawing of a left turn, then a right turn, then some more left turns and a right, all with street names squeezed in to fit into the right places. At the end of the map was a cross and 'Grovesnor Square, 7 pm' in capital letters. "Leave the cabinet and wait here," another cross indicated a little side street. Mark knew Grovesnor Square and it was not somewhere he wanted to be at 7 pm.

He searched each room for his mobile, finding it on the toilet cistern. "Of course that's where you'd be," Mark said aloud, "it makes perfect sense." He found Karina's number.

"Hi love," she gushed, "everything alright?" He knew she meant 'have you gotten rid of all the stuff I don't like yet.'

"Fine, um, did you send me a present? A...really weird present?"

"No, when? What do you mean?"

"I just got this thing from the postman..." he paused, unsure suddenly of mentioning such an unpleasant street to his sweet girlfriend. If she thought he had anything to do with unsavoury things she might change her mind about letting him move in, and his lease would be up and he'd have nowhere to go but a tiny box room... or worse. "It's nothing, just some chain thing. I thought you might have signed me up for something as a joke."

"Of course not," she chuckled. "All set for next week?"

"Yep," he said, hating himself for lying. Her colleague, Tarquin or Maximillian or something equally annoying, piped up in the background asking if she was up for getting thoroughly jollied at Chi-Chi's later. Mark's lips pursed so tightly they almost burst.

"You know I can't afford that place."

"I know, I wasn't going to say yes," her voice was sharp, defensive, "I can't help people asking."

Mark imagined her going without him, throwing her head back at Tarquin's jokes, downing shots, her leaning against him as she got tipsy. Tarquin would promise to get her home safe, holding her close as he called her a cab. Mark knew she would never betray him but couldn't help the way his mind slid down the rabbit hole, "I know. Look," he couldn't believe what he was doing. He mentally punched himself in the face as the words fell out, "if you want to go, you should go. I can get on with sorting things out here."

"Oh my God, really? Thank you Mark, you're the best. I love you!" She was gone, maybe forever. Mark stared at his phone. Had she even said goodbye? What had he done? He sloped back to list more items on Ebay and watch them not sell. His week off work was almost over and he was nowhere near ready to move to such a fancy part of town. He'd have to borrow money. Who from? He couldn't ask his parents again, they had nothing. His anus prolapsed at the thought. Sending CVs to better jobs was going nowhere. Maybe he could get a loan…

His eyes wandered to the map. What could it mean? He turned it over and over, checked the box for the company name: Red Tower LTD Mystery Packages. He typed the name into the internet and brought up a very ordinary, basic website, but couldn't find any contact information. He dialled directory enquiries, "who?" said the lady on the other end. He repeated the name and listened to her frantic typing, "Sorry, can't find anything. Can I help you with anything else?"

"No," said Mark, a funny feeling in his belly, "its fine, thanks."

Four O'clock came and Mark made his quarter hour check on Ebay. A cushion had sold for ten pounds, but none of the big items. He sighed and fell back onto the sofa. Six O'clock came and he hadn't moved. Six thirty. He nibbled on a slice of fresh white bread, the only luxury he could afford right now. He picked up the map, shifting from foot to foot. Before he could second guess himself, he was out the door with the cabinet and marching towards Grovesnor Square.

The light had long since faded and the street lamps were few and far between. Grovesnor Square was as full of sordid and desperate characters as he expected; men in threadbare coats hissing their class A wares, women in very little waiting for men in cars and all eyeing his pockets, judging his wealth, evidently deciding that mugging him would be too much effort for too little reward. He checked the map, left the cabinet on the corner of the street and snuck into the shadows of a nearby alley.

His fingers and lips burned with cold. Whoever had sent him the map was probably watching him right now and having a good laugh. He went to stand, his knees cracking and back aching, when he spotted a stooped old man shuffling towards the cabinet with something in his arms. Quickly he lowered himself again and watched as the man placed whatever it was he carried onto the top shelf—it looked like old books—and just stared. Mark couldn't fathom it. The old man stood there for several minutes until another man arrived, also carrying a pile of books. He grumbled something to the other but Mark couldn't make out his words, though he understood when the first grabbed his goods and scurried away. The newcomer also heaved his armful into the spot where the old man's had been. Instead of just staring, though, he rubbed an admiring hand over the wood, back and forth, again and again. Mark had to admit it was good quality wood, the cabinet had cost a fair bit, but what was happening?

On and on this went, more and more people showing up until there was a queue. Most waited their turn patiently but occasionally an argument or scuffle broke out, Mark overhearing "my turn," and "don't be so selfish." During these moments he fidgeted, should he do something? Was it his fault if old men tore each other apart over his cabinet? The other inhabitants of Grovesnor Square barely looked their way, as if they'd seen the same thing many times. This calmed Mark somewhat, though not completely.

Finally the sun came up and Mark, by now sitting with his back to the wall and knees drawn up for warmth, pulled himself to his feet groaning. He was only just thirty but every part of his body hurt. He limped to the cabinet, occupied by a single young man in a green cardigan and thick, unfashionable trousers. The pimps, the prostitutes and the dealers had long gone and the floor was a sea of fish and chip wrappers and condom packets. The man didn't notice Mark until he was right next to him, his eyes widening to a horrific size. He stumbled back, "Sorry, sorry." He grabbed his tome from the shelf and speed walked with hunched shoulders to safety. Mark watched for a while, head shaking in confusion, and glanced at the top shelf.

"Fuck!" There, just waiting to live in his pocket, was a pile of notes; twenties, tens, fivers, all for him. His hand shook as he stuffed them away and bent his knees to grab the most wonderful cabinet in the world. He shrieked when a hand landed on his shoulder.

"Sorry," said a plain looking woman in glasses and a pink cotton dress, "I did call but you were in your own world." Mark went to speak but she cut him off, "I want your cabinet."

"What?"

"We need it at the library," she tilted her head, perhaps in an effort to seem earnest, "it's the one in Marlborough Street, do you know it?"

"Yes," it was a nice library and ran lots of projects to encourage children to read. Mark's hand went to the notes in his pocket, "can I see some library ID?"

The woman's demeanour crumbled, "OK, fine, I'm not with the library, but I'll make sure you're well compensated. How does £2,000 sound?"

"I don't know." He stared at his feet. If this woman was so eager to buy clearly he'd get a lot more than a measly two thousand out of it, "maybe try Ebay? There's bound to be others."

The woman's smile was tight, she was losing patience, "yes, there are, but they don't have the craftsmanship this one does. Can't you feel that?" she rubbed her hand down the knotted side, "that's a genuine Leminski." Mark again mentally punched himself for not taking it to auction. Perhaps he would once he got rid of this crazy person. "Just to see your books on one of these shelves for ten minutes is a... privilege...not easily forgotten." Mark didn't like the shivery, ecstatic way she uttered the last few words. The entire thing felt slimy.

"Fine, I'll let you know if I come across any other Lemski's," he picked up the cabinet and turned to leave.

"Leminski," growled the woman. Mark wanted to laugh at her seriousness but something primal warned him against it. He knew she had a gun before he turned to face her, "Hand it over." He placed the cabinet on the ground and backed slowly away. "That's it," she murmured, "right over there." He watched helplessly as she picked it up and placed it in a car without taking her eyes off him, getting into the front seat and driving off.

Mark watched the road for a long time after she had left.

He spent the morning pacing up and down the flat. Perhaps it wasn't such a big deal. Fifty pounds was OK, it wasn't a lot but it showed he was capable of making money. And then sponging from his girlfriend until she went off with someone less destitute and he lost his job because he was depressed and ended up living in a pavement crack begging for change. He slumped in the chair and checked his phone – no calls. He checked facebook – practically a wall of Karina and her new best friend Tarquin, or whatever his name was. In one picture they clinked glasses. In another they danced against each other. In another they stagily puckered their lips for a kiss. Sick churned in Mark's stomach but he couldn't stop looking. Eventually he slammed his phone onto the table and stormed to the computer.

He typed Leminski and brought up an advert. Someone, he assumed the woman from earlier, had announced ten minutes ago on Gumtree and other platforms that a "high quality, magnificently crafted item was just waiting to "groan beneath your possessions for one pound a minute. Got a first edition Edgar Allen Poe? Bring it here. Brand new, leather bound Sylvia Plath? Don't hesitate." Below was an address. Mark snorted humorlessly before making his way to the boxes in the back room and pulling out a baseball bat. He went to snatch his phone before charging out into the street and it beeped: Karina. "Hey babe, U OK? How's boxing up goin? Miss U." He stared at it for several minutes, looked up at the door and back at the phone again. Karina would wrap him in love and kisses and his money troubles would dissipate like a bath bomb. But then, once he broke free of her arms, they would return. He gripped the bat.

On the street Mark tried to look as if he might be going to play a wholesome baseball game rather than the thing he was actually on his way to do, unaware that his fixed grin made him look even more menacing. He had scrawled the address on a piece of paper but the words were scorched into his memory, and he marched until he arrived on a road punctuated by leafy trees and healthy children. "Baseball!" shouted one child, pointing in hope at Mark. His sister, or friend, shushed him, sensing danger.

Her front door was surprisingly normal for a cabinet hijacker. Mark pressed the buzzer of the Victorian terrace and, when she answered through the intercom, made sure he spoke in a breathy voice, "I heard you have a Leminski."

"Yes, my, you're quick off the mark. Just a moment." He heard footsteps down the stairs and the door opened. Mark checked to see if she still had a gun. Nothing. At first she smiled blankly, but realisation pooled a split second before he cracked her in the face. Mark blocked out the children's screams and plunged upstairs.

"Now…uh…hang on," blubbed a man in a luxurious dressing gown in the tasteful front room.

"Hang on this," yelled Mark, feeling like a vigilante

in a 80s action movie. He spied the cabinet and grabbed it, yelping in surprise when a teenage girl launched herself at him. She must have been in the next room. He yanked her up by the hair and kicked her in the stomach, leaving her moaning on the floor as he dashed out with his prize.

He didn't get three yards before the police were on him, knocking him to his front, blocking his windpipe and cramping his legs. "No!" he wailed as his arm was twisted from the cabinet to join the other behind his back, "She stole my cabinet, I wanted my cabinet." His screeches tore through the neighbourhood, and children cried and laughed and danced with nervous excitement, and grown-ups shook their heads and put their hands to their mouths, and Mark was stuffed into the car and the cabinet removed for 'evidence.' A week later it surfaced on the same street corner, an off-duty policeman watching from the shadows.

7

The seventh parcel arrived at a small bedsit in a building block in the city.

Nicky wished she could shove the mop up his arse. She pictured it bursting from his mouth while he struggled like a skewered pig. Maybe she would make a bad pun like an 80s action hero, "watch where you sit," or "you look rushed off your feet." No, those didn't work.

"Hello?" he said, snapping her back into the office. He grinned as though she were a dog doing back flips - badly. She looked down at the spot he said she'd missed and mopped it grimly. The only other worker in at that time, another man maybe ten years her junior, shot her an apologetic look and she smiled back, grateful. "Only 'avin' a laugh," said the first. Nicky grunted, knowing that sulking would encourage him but unable to access a more mature response.

The toilets were shitty, the urinals pissy and the bin was filled with mold, but she threw herself into the task with a soft sigh and found, as she had the day before and the day before that, she enjoyed the satisfaction of getting it clean, that the hypnotic movement of scrubbing and mopping soothed her and, when it was done, she felt an immense pride that she hadn't for much of her life. Sometimes she thought of Skye and what she'd say if she saw Nicky now—probably make some derisive comment or, worse, look at her with pity—but Nicky was happy. It was only ruined when other people tore through her bubble.

She tied the plastic bag and heaved it to the bins, determined as always to prove that she might be tiny but she could cope, she belonged there. A delivery van had pulled up and the driver was chatting with Loudmouth, who had left the warmth of the office to sign for whatever had arrived. Nicky ignored them both and pushed against the dumpster lid. It wouldn't budge. She shoved, hard, and eventually it creaked into life. She clumsily threw the bin inside, noticing the amused glance pass between the men. She pursed her lips furiously.

Back at home, she flung herself on the couch. This was the dangerous time. Working so early meant she had a large portion of evening in which to avoid taking heroin. She switched on the TV and relaxed under the familiar gaze of the presenters chatting with a celebrity about their latest magnum opus, listening to her stomach gurgle. After the truly terrible part of initially coming off drugs, the worst part for her was how wet her body was. Never mind the tedium of everyday, never mind the weird aches and pains she couldn't medicate just in case, what really disturbed her was how gloopy her organs felt, like a garden bursting with life after a long winter. She missed her safe, dry heroin body. Now she felt on the edge of shitting herself or otherwise leaking fluid like an alien rejecting its human host.

She noticed the package, bringing it back to the sofa. If Brian or Skye had sent her drugs she wouldn't be able to throw them away. She knew she couldn't. In response her back hurt, a new complaint from hours of bending at work. When she saw that it wasn't drugs she cursed herself for hoping that it was. She studied the slip of paper at the bottom of the box. There were just two questions and, opposite each, 'tick for yes or cross for no' above two boxes. After a while she grabbed a pen from the kitchen, took a meal from the freezer and placed it in the microwave. She read the questions again, "Do you crave a change? Would you do anything to start a new life?" and ticked 'yes' after each, then threw the paper in the bin. As always, she fell asleep on the sofa with the TV on.

She was on time, as always. It was still dark and the only lights in the industrial cul-de-sac glowed from the windows. She knocked on the back door…nothing. No, not again. She couldn't have her pay docked again. She banged, so hard that the door vibrated. "Alright," bellowed a warehouse man as he flung the door open, "you don't have to bang so fucking loud."

"Alright," Nicky snapped. The man continued shouting as he wandered away, "I can't even hear what you're saying."

"Get your fucking ears cleaned then."

"Oh, fuck off," Nicky stormed to the cleaning cupboard and shut the door. Hot tears burst from her eyes and she wiped them angrily away. She'd done it again. She didn't want to be that person anymore and she hated herself for it and hated that man for bringing it out of her. Surely she couldn't stay after that. She waited but nobody came to speak to her, bad news or otherwise. After several long seconds she emerged and clocked in, doing her routine, waiting to be fired but it never happened. When it was over she scuttled to freedom, praying she wouldn't be locked out the next morning.

Back at home there was another box by the door. No writing, just as before. She cut off the sellotape and pulled out a little black velvet box. Neon blue words above a small hole read "Give us your hand." She peeked inside but saw nothing. She wasn't about to stick her hand into an unknown space, was she? Quickly, before she could change her mind, she took the plunge. She blinked, and when her eyes opened she was in an endless, black landscape. She was too afraid to feel fear; instead a guttural need to escape pounded through her body. She tried to move her feet but barely twitched a muscle.

"Ah, you're here," said a voice neither male nor

female, "nice and prompt." Nicky turned to see a rainbow figure sitting at a desk, its hair a pink cloud of cotton candy. When she tried to work out its features she was hit by a veil of confusion. "To the desk, please," it gestured for her to come nearer. Nicky obliged, her fear retreating into nauseous disquiet. "That's lovely," it smiled. "We're offering you the position on a trial basis depending on how you deal with the next task. Have you ever harvested fluff before?"

"Huh?"

"Of course not. If you'll just gather up the balls and place them in this basket, we'll discuss regular hours," it handed her a wicker basket with a handle.

Nicky didn't have time to question further before the darkness cleared to her left, revealing a square patch of grey, twisted trees in clumpy earth – no, not earth, people, hairless and shrunken, lying on their backs in neat rows, branches sprouting from their bellies. On the ends of their knotted boughs sprouted black apples with the consistency of smoke, but when Nicky approached them and squeezed one it yielded to her touch easily – fluff. Bemused, she pulled it from the stalk, eliciting a grunt from the man below. Horror and self-disgust spasmed through her when she realised it may have hurt him.

"They're fine," said the desk worker, "please continue." Blocking out the soft whimpers and moans, Nicky's basket filled quickly, and when the last was harvested she handed it over. "Wonderful," it said, "good job."

Nicky was about to ask what was happening and if she could go home when she woke on the sofa. Disappointment flooded her and, like always, she wished she had some drugs. Instead she made tea, pouring the boiling water into the cup when she noticed a piece of paper on the kitchen table. She called it the kitchen table, but the bedsit didn't have clearly defined rooms, only designated areas. However it was nearer the oven than anywhere else, therefore it was the kitchen table. She studied the paper and made a noise like a confused dog. "Hours, Wages," it said in two columns on the left. "Two, 100 pounds" it said on the right. She threw it, watching it flutter to her feet, stubbornly real. That was more than she earned in a week in her real job. If only it was real, rather than a delayed withdrawal nightmare. Still, she couldn't help wondering what would happen if she tried to put it in her account. Chuckling mischievously, she tucked it into her purse and grabbed her coat.

In the queue it didn't seem like such a good idea. What if they thought she was trying to defraud them and the police were called? They'd put her away this time and everything she'd built up would crumble. Hands sweating, she handed it to the clerk, "sorry, I might have got it wrong, I'm not sure," she babbled, but the teller barely glanced at it.

"Card, please?"

"Um, yes." Shifting from foot to foot, she watched the teller punch in the numbers and hand her back the card. "Thank you," she whispered, rushing outside to check her balance. It was there, 100 pounds, plus the 60 already there. "What?" Nicky pulled out her phone to buy drugs, then realised she didn't actually want any. She wanted to go shopping instead, which she did with a glorious abandon. Jumpers, a coat, new dresses, she hadn't had such things for years. Most of her possessions were lost either from being abandoned in a hurry or pinched by other junkies, including those who were supposed to be her best friends. Of course, she had done exactly the same. No longer, for the first time she knew the craving had stopped.

When her alarm tore through the dark morning, Nicky rolled over with a moan. She got out of bed feeling like she'd had no rest at all, which she hadn't if her dream was reality. She charged to work, trying to fight the frost with movement, but she was still shivering when she knocked on the door. No answer. Oh God, not again. Her clocking in time evaporated in the cold air as she knocked again and again. Finally Loudmouth emerged for a cigarette, "You're a bit late, aren't you?" She bit her lip, desperately swallowing a torrent of abuse.

All through the rest of her shift she yelled at them in her head. She shoved the hoover and mop into nooks and crannies, imagining the breaking spider webs and crumbling dust were brains and faces. As always she didn't say goodbye on her way out.

There was another cheque on the table on her return.

She opened the window and leaned out, wondering if she would catch her provider disappearing down the street. There was nobody except for a young mother wheeling her pushchair while a toddler dawdled behind. She shut it and studied the paper, grinning like a madwoman. It was the same as before. She stuffed it into her coat pocket and darted back out the door – she should put it safe in her bank. While she was in town she could get some much needed supplies, just for the room. And a coat. And a new bag. But after that she should definitely save. And maybe a hat.

The horizon was as black and impenetrable as before. The desk clerk paused while filing their nails, smiling as Nicky approached. "Wonderful," they said briskly, draining the word of all meaning, "we've some handles that need turning." They pointed to an enormous crank on the side of a long pole above a circular void.

"Yup," Nicky tried to supress a grin, this work was so easy. She turned, reminding herself whenever her arms ached how much money she'd be getting for so little. The desk clerk had returned to the nail file, occasionally staring into the distance. Nicky's mind wandered. What was down there? She strained her eyes until finally she could make something out, something tiny, almost a pin prick. It was a creature, not human but definitely living, doing a strange dance. No…not a dance. She squinted. It was on a table which was getting longer, and those strange movements were attempts to break free. Oh God…it was on a rack…which she was turning. The creature's blue fur was matted with blood and its little paws were twisted with broken digits. Its big eyes were squeezed in agony. Its ears were very similar to a rabbits but one appeared to have been torn half off. She could just about hear its high pitched squeal like a dog toy being trodden on.

"Keep going, please," said the desk clerk. Nicky hadn't realised she'd stopped, but now she gazed at the handle as though it was a diseased syringe, "please continue." Her hands shaking, Nicky gripped it lightly and tried to turn it as softly as she could, but it was useless, without enough power it didn't turn at all. She calculated her choices in her head: she could leave and go back to her cleaning wage as the only source of income, or she could turn. Perhaps, she thought as she resumed her task, she could complete tonight's job and go for help in the morning. Deciding on that, she threw herself into her work.

The alarm screamed and she yelped. Once she remembered who and where she was, the tiny tortured figure came back to her. The idea of going for help, which last night had seemed so important, now seemed like the fastest way into the loony bin. She'd only just finished parole, there was no way she was going back under supervision of any kind. She dressed solemnly.

She sighed as she pushed open the door. It was quiet, only one or two of the men who said a friendly hello and left her alone were in. Grateful, she heaved the hoover from the cleaning cupboard into the office and plugged it in. Flicking the switch, she aimed the nozzle at a pile of dust and…nothing. It wasn't picking up. She tried it elsewhere and still nothing. "Fuck you," she whispered under her breath. At that moment the outside door slammed and in came Loudmouth and his crony. "Alright," they both said, destroying the calm morning. "What you doing?"

"Just, I don't know, it's not working."

"You've gotta change the bag, you pillock."

"I do? Is that my job?" Nicky couldn't look at them. Shame at not knowing such a simple thing roared through her and stopped her thinking clearly.

"Course it is."

"You're the cleaner."

"You're a mental."

On and on they went, a boy either side, a howling cacophony of derision. They cackled and grinned but Nicky wasn't in on the joke. She looked up desperately, hoping the line manager was there. He was, and he was laughing too. "OK," she threw the hoover down, "fine." She stormed out and grabbed her coat from the office.

"Wait," one of the boys called after her.

"Only having a laugh," said the other, but she kept going. Once outside, she hugged herself with glee.

8

The eighth parcel arrived at a house share on a nice
leafy street in the city. The recipient – Mary, a student
of French and Spanish – gingerly opened it as though
expecting a jack-in-the-box to pop out. Inside was a
rusty key which she turned over and over, waiting for
an explanation, none forthcoming until she looked
back up at the white wall between the front room and
the kitchen and saw a wooden door beside the original.
It was dark mahogany with an ornate key hole and,
once Mary got over the initial shock, she was a little
disappointed that it didn't match the rest of the house.
Binah, her housemate who studied Biology, barged
in from her bedroom carrying a tin box, "I don't use
this. It takes up too much room. Do you want..." she
paused, looking from the door to Mary and back again.
"What the hell is that?"

"I don't know..." Mary pressed against it, "it's real."

She paused, wondering what the next move should be. "My dad always said I can solve any problem. I've always been able to think logically about anything." If she'd glanced to her left during her assertion she would have noticed Binah, ever so slightly, perhaps even unaware she was doing it, mouthing along with her.

"I think," said Binah, "we should just open it."

"We can't, we ought to take a step back and think about this properly."

"OK, let's think. What should we do instead?"

Mary opened her mouth then closed it again. She ran her hands over the door frame, wondering what her logical self would do. She sighed and inserted the key into the lock, studiously avoiding Binah's probable smug face. The door creaked open, revealing darkness. If it wanted her to step inside, it was going the wrong way about it.

"Go on then."

"I am." Finally they linked arms and they stepped as one into the void.

It looked like the lobby of a spacious hotel. An unoccupied check in desk stood beside a grand set of stairs, and corridors led to various closed doors. The girls exchanged a look and Binah made her way to the desk, picking up a sheet of white paper. Mary watched helplessly, willing herself to move, replaying the scene in her head with herself as the more take charge one. With hunched shoulders she followed Binah's footsteps. The paper appeared to be some kind of menu, the words

'Hope Palace' in elegant, looping silver letters at the top, but something was oddly familiar about the list beneath it. She squeaked involuntarily, trying to make sense of it. "What?" Binah scrutinized her face.

"I recognise those," Mary pointed to the options, which weren't meals at all. 'Lady Time,' proclaimed the first, with smaller letters beneath describing it as "a podcast where women discuss any and all topics, from current events to places to eat." The podcast name, which at one point had seemed like a clever play on her Nan's nickname for periods, glared back at her accusingly. "I mean, that wasn't the final title I settled on. I had a few, I just wrote that down as a placeholder."

"What was it?"

"Oh," Mary screwed up her face, "it was an idea of Julie's, remember her? I said I'd help with her podcast but I ended up doing the whole thing because none of it made sense when she showed me her notes." She hid her blush by looking at the next item, Crash Course. Her intestines melted with embarrassment when she remembered the comedy web series she had started with her old school friends on YouTube. The comments had been so mean! People were jealous. A flicker of regret told her she shouldn't have given up on it. It was good.

"These are your ideas. This is great," Binah gripped Mary's shoulder, "you're always going on about how you wish you were doing side projects again, we should look in on a few and you can take notes or something."

Mary wanted to say no, that she wouldn't have time

what with her lessons and all, but the sense of dread she felt went beyond not having time. She couldn't place it, she just knew she didn't want to go. "Come on," Binah seemed confused, "you can always learn from them if they're not good. First ideas are never…"

"They were good," Mary snapped, instantly regretting it. Why did she feel like a sausage threatening to burst through its skin? She knew her ideas were good. She'd spent every evening alone scribbling, window closed against the yells and cackles of drunken revellers. Of course her ideas were good, "OK, let's go."

They arrived at the nearest door, which had a small gold plaque with Lady Time neatly emblazoned. Mary, with almost undetectable hesitation, pushed it open. The pair found themselves in a radio studio not unlike something they'd seen on TV. Three women sat around a table wearing headsets and talking into microphones, one dressed in a power suit, another in an expensive looking dress and the third in a cosy but smart sweater and trousers. "Welcome, listeners, to another episode of Lady Time," said the first woman, "I'm joined today by Olympian Anna Meryl."

"What sport does she do?" Binah frowned. Mary couldn't explain that she'd made her up because she knew nothing about sport, including an entire transcript between the hosts and the imaginary woman. She was going to look into the finer details of who to interview and what to ask at a later stage, but she'd been too busy to get the project off the ground.

"I can't remember," she whispered.

"So, Anna," said the third woman, "what can you tell us about being in sport?"

"It isn't easy," the second woman smiled winningly, "but I practice a lot."

Binah snorted, covering her mouth sheepishly. Mary's face blazed, "let's get out of here, this is no good." Mary burst from the room, feeling as though she'd revealed her most disgusting secret only for everyone to point and laugh. Her ribcage hurt beneath the violence of her heart. Binah followed, continuing to giggle idiotically, stopping only when she noticed her friend's discomfort.

The next room was a quirky health food café with walls covered in art and streamers. Four ultra-cool looking girls sat at a table, chatting and laughing. "This is the web series I planned out during my A levels," Mary gushed. She hadn't strictly planned it out except in her head, but she knew basically exactly how it would go. A ball of pride formed in her chest on seeing it as a reality. She held her breath to keep from crying.

A young, attractive man approached the girls, looking straight at the one with dark curly hair, "hey, I saw you over there, I was wondering if I could have your number?"

"Oh, were you?" said the girl. The others tutted and stood up, gathering their bags and coats, grumbling about male egos.

"Look," he held his hands up, "I didn't mean any disrespect."

By then the other girls had left. Curly haired girl reached into her pocket and pulled out a card, "here you go, don't tell them," she whispered before rushing out. Mary and Binah headed for the café door to follow them onto the street.

"That wasn't bad," Binah sounded a little impressed, but mainly surprised. Mary decided not to take the bait. After a few more steps, though, she couldn't help herself.

"What do you mean, not bad? I thought it was funny."

"Well, yeah, I mean it was, but there's a few bits that need tidying. I mean, people that age don't carry cards, and…"

"They do, I've been handed cards." The urge to cry returned, only this time it was definitely not from happiness. Mary couldn't be in that room anymore. The walls dripped with accusations and the breath wouldn't leave her body. She stormed out, trying not to hyperventilate, wishing that Binah would just go away.

"Let's try across the hall," Binah marched towards another door, trying to pretend she wasn't covering her mouth against laughter. Mary wished her mother was there to give the silly girl a piece of her mind. Everyone at college was so immature. She was too used to adult conversation. Her father had always said she was grown up from a very young age.

Binah opened the door and went inside. Mary watched, her feet not moving. As long as she was out here she was safe. Like Binah knew how to do anything creative, anyway. She was a scientist, all she knew was equations. But then, when she pictured going home without seeing her work realised, she knew she had to face it. The plaque on the door read "Business Tactics."

The office was the kind of shiny, corporate building Mary had always pictured herself working. People would ask her questions, nod when she spoke in meetings and eventually, after proving herself, she'd make it to the top. She had already picked out what cushions she wanted for the chair at her desk, not that she could share that with the other students. She knew it wouldn't be easy but she'd always been determined. She surveyed the scene – two women at their desks, one glancing furtively at the other's computer. "Hey," said the other, "stop trying to steal my ideas."

"I am not."

"You are. I caught you. That's it," she rose from her seat and fetched a clipboard, balancing it beside her computer, blocking the other girl's view, "I can't risk you humiliating me in front of Mr Carver again."

What was this? This had been a biting corporate drama when she'd envisioned it as a TV pilot last year, with tense, interweaving storylines and warts and all characters. She hadn't written this. The script was terrible, the acting was off. Why was the acting bad? Were they making fun of her? "This is useless," she gripped the door handle.

"Wait," Binah said, "why don't we make notes? Use them to make it better? Come on," she grabbed a pen and paper from the desk, the workers either not caring or unable to see them.

"This isn't what I wrote," fumed Mary, knowing full well it was. It was this place. It was twisting her words, making them ridiculous. Of course it would sound bad here, the actors weren't even trying. Binah scribbled furiously onto the page, clearly trying not to erupt into cackles. "What are you doing?"

"It's given me an idea."

"Oh, it has, has it?" Binah's head snapped up at her companion's sharp tone, "for a comedy, I suppose?"

"Well…"

"You're in this with them, aren't you?"

All traces of humour disappeared from Binah, "no, what do you…"

"I suppose you'll be telling everyone you thought my ideas were crap. Well, I hope you enjoyed yourself, you're always bullying me." Mary couldn't stop, the words kept exploding. She'd had enough. She was tired of being the nice one, the one that helped everybody with their college work, the one that did all the cleaning. It was time Binah and the others knew they couldn't treat people that way, "good luck finding another roommate, I'm moving out tomorrow." Binah gaped as if she'd just witnessed a person setting themselves on fire. Mary didn't care, tomorrow she'd write the best play ever about all she'd endured and they'd all be sorry.

9

The ninth parcel arrived at a high rise council flat. Craig dragged his feet indoors, trying not to think about the terrible night he'd had trying to talk to people. When he was a boy he'd cried at every birthday party and his mother, god rest her, couldn't figure out why, until just before his seventh birthday when he asked her why people had to have them when they were so horrible. Shocked, she'd hugged him and said, "You don't have to. I had no idea." From then on he was party free and it was wonderful. In the following years, though, all his friends were throwing engagement parties and work promotion parties and someone flushed the loo well parties. Sometimes Craig used his Retinitis Pigmantosa as an excuse but he couldn't every time. Night blindness and tunnel vision might make it harder to get about but the truth was that he just didn't like people. No, he did like people; he just didn't like it when they congregated together, and anyone who didn't go to their parties apparently wasn't a proper friend despite being there through break-ups and hard times. When his oldest and closest friend Matt had an operation and lost his father at the same time Craig had practically lived at his house for a month, cooking and taking care of him, but now Matt had met Sarah and her fancy new friends and that was that.

He opened the package in the kitchen with a pair of scissors, thinking about the slice of cake he'd brought back with him. Tony was marrying Elizabeth (not Liz) and he'd have to attend the wedding next June despite barely being able to stand her. He'd noticed her withering looks at his outfit but he'd done his best, dammit. He couldn't help it if his job only gave him enough to shop second hand – not that he could have told her that.

A pamphlet lay at the bottom of the parcel. Bemused, he picked it up and held it close: How To Win Friends And Have A Jolly Time. He snorted, it had to have been sent to the wrong person. When he began to flick through, however, something ran up his spine. It was crazy, it could never be taken seriously. "Whether it's a birthday party, a Halloween party or just a gathering of friends for a gay time, it takes planning," he could clearly hear the fifties educational film voice, "if you want to be a whizz at the next bash follow these words to the letter and you're sure to be a hit. We'll guide you from shopping for gladrags to saying your last farewell. You need never be a sad sack again." He read and re-read the first step, wondering which of his friends had gone to the trouble of putting this together and posting it. It had to be Ben, it was exactly the kind of thing he and his office friends would do. He chuckled and lay on the couch to watch TV. Ben was going to be at Matt's swanky get together next week, maybe he'd show him and really follow through with his advice.

Saturday morning came and Craig flipped to the first page, shopping for clothes. "Fetch a hot new number straight off the rack," it said, "A few suggestions would be a glittering unitard, some real fur with the head still attached, an unfunny costume or perhaps some offensive make up." Craig had an idea of what the offensive make up would be and decided to forego it, but he flipped out his blind stick and made his way to town to see what he could rustle up. If all went well, he might be excused from all parties in future without it being his fault, he could just blame Ben.

He picked out a tampon with armholes in the Costume Shop. It was everything Craig found annoying and the kind of tacky thing that would mortify Matt. He brought it to the cashier, expecting snickers. "Good choice, sir," he said, appraising it as though it were a fine suit, "you've picked from our higher end range. I'll get that bagged up for you."

Craig turned to the next page, "It's mighty bad manners to turn up to a party without bringing a present. Most people will select a beverage, but which one is suitable? Forget your fancy wines, this calls for store brand Orangeade."

Tampon outfit on and Orangeade in full view, he pressed Matt's door buzzer and waited for the horrorshow to begin. The bottle was slipping a little from the nervous sweat on his palms, but there was no way he was going to let them see his discomfort. Sarah answered the door and he saw himself from the outside, wishing bitterly he'd made a genuine effort. He didn't want anyone to think he'd lost his mind or, worse, found this kind of thing funny. Also...just for a second...he felt bad for her. She organises a nice party and her boyfriend's grouchy friend decides to have a joke at her expense. He turned to leave when Sarah hooted, "Craig, don't you look fancy?" He gave an awkward little laugh. His eyes hadn't adjusted enough to see her expression but it sounded like she was taking it well. "Where did you get that outfit? It looks so expensive. Matt, your friend's here!"

He allowed himself to be led to the main throng who stood about the front room in small groups chatting about work or childhood memories, or next year's plans, or any other safe subject. Craig was sneaking a peek at the pamphlet's next page on conversations when Matt embraced him as if they'd escaped an island together. "It's been too long," he said, his mouth muffled in the string part of Craig's costume.

"I did call you last week." Craig squeezed his eyes

shut, why did he have to be so antagonistic? It just fell out of his mouth.

"I'll call you in the week, I promise," said Matt graciously. He stepped back to take in his friend, "well, look at you. You're doing well I see." Craig shrugged, embarrassed. "I'll go get us a drink, I'd like you to meet some of my colleagues," he guided him to a small group including a short woman and two attractive men, all very smart and well-groomed. Craig was having second thoughts on following the pamphlet's advice, the last thing he wanted was to actually upset anyone, but when they delivered bone crushing handshakes he no longer cared.

"James, right?" James nodded his head, "I heard you're looking to get the sand in your vagina removed next week?"

"I can't believe you actually remembered, it must be three months since I last met you," James gripped Craig's arm in a masculine show of friendship. "So, Craig, how's life treating you?" Craig's brain crackled with questions. What were they hearing? It couldn't be the words actually coming from his mouth.

"Oh, you know, same old routine; gnaw the heads off some chickens, smear myself in feces and summon the dark ones."

"Good man," the arm squeeze turned into a back slap.

"I'm not bread, you don't have to massage me."

"This guy," James almost had tears in his eyes from laughter. The other man, too, was having a whale of a time. Only the girl didn't look too impressed.

"I'd better check up on that drink," said Craig, backing towards the kitchen. Matt was leaning against the fridge, very close to a red haired girl Craig had seen at previous parties. She was downcast, hurt, while Matt placated. They were whispering as seriously as relatives at a hospice and, when Craig entered, their eyes snapped up guiltily.

"Hey," said Matt, looking as though he was praying for an asteroid.

"Who's your friend?" said the red head.

"Nobody," Matt seemed peeved at the way she was eyeing him. "Uh, an old friend," he caught Craig's look of irritation, "from the estate."

"The estate?" She seemed confused, "you don't look like you live on an estate," she rubbed the tampon felt. She must really want to upset Matt.

"I don't, I live in a bucket by the M6."

"Oh," Matt's eyes narrowed with jealousy, "you moved then?"

"Why don't we go somewhere quieter and have a proper chat," the girl led him by the elbow. Craig hesitated, studying Matt's tight lips and folded arms. He may be a cheating bastard with a condescending girlfriend but he was still a friend. On the other hand, perhaps he could talk this girl out of weeks of misery. He followed her to the bedroom where she closed the door, sat on the bed and burst into tears.

"Sorry," she snuffled, "I made you think you were getting lucky."

"No," Craig sat beside her, "Look, these people are a bunch of cunts. I mean, some are alright, but only because I've known them so long. Find yourself someone outside this circle, someone nice."

She sloppily wiped her eyes and nose and smiled at him, "you're such a smooth talker. How do you always know what to say?" Craig shrugged. "Thanks," she hugged him, "I'm gonna go home now." Craig guided her through the throng, trying to shield her from the daggers shooting from Sarah's eyes. "Bye," said the girl as she disappeared into the night, waving like a child. Craig waved back.

"Seeing off your first conquest already?" said a voice dryly. Craig turned, eventually seeing the woman from the first group in the porch, sarcastic eyebrow raised.

"Eh? No."

"Don't worry, I won't mention her to the next one."

"Look, I don't know what sort of bloke you think I am, but I'm not like that."

"Of course not, that's why you just came out the bedroom."

"I don't have to explain myself," he barged past.

The front room was filled with bodies jerking to the rhythm of the 80s hits now blasting from the speakers. Craig had always hated dancing but curiosity got the better of him and he followed the instructions, flailing like a semaphore sender in fast forward. A crowd gathered around him, cheering and clapping, and Craig kept spinning, beginning to feel as though he might actually enjoy himself. His hand slapped hard against something and his eyes darted about, trying to locate it, finally settling on Sarah rubbing her cheek. "Fuck, sorry."

"It's OK," she half purred, half whimpered, blinking away tears and sliding towards him, "keep dancing."

"Um…"

"Come on," she slid a hand around his back and pushed, attempting to lead him but succeeding only in making him fall. He caught Matt's expression on the way down, his fury revealing Sarah's motive.

"Right, that's it," Craig stood up, "I've had enough. I am gonna go home and don't ever invite me to one of your arsehole conventions again." He pulled the tampon head off and the entire room gasped in horror. "Sorry," he said, "I didn't mean you were arseholes. You're not. I-just-I'm going home."

He shuffled through the crowd, their eyes as wide as their mouths. Sarah folded her arms, "Yes, quite right, time you left." Craig opened his mouth to retort, deciding against it and continuing towards the door. Matt was now by her side, united in their hatred of the man in the tampon.

"Wait for me," said a female voice. A hand rested on his back and he turned to see the girl from earlier, eyebrow no longer raised. "There's a pub round the corner, fancy a pint?"

"Sounds good," they linked arms, and Craig stuffed the pamphlet into a bin on the way out.

EPILOGUE

The stool where Kapoor had sat was still empty from yesterday and the workroom was glum. A sharp pain tore through Sprouse's wrist as he reached for the box in front of him. He kept his expression admirably blank and tried to lighten the mood, "anyone remember that guy with the guitar? What was his name? Song about cleaning windows or something? And a stick of Blackpool rock?"

"Not a guitar," Smith's brow knitted together, "a little thing, sounded all tinny."

"Yeah, that's right," said Jefferson from the conveyer belt behind. Others chimed in and the atmosphere again erupted. It didn't do to dwell on the negative. Instead they grasped at whatever memories they could pull from the fog of their lives before The Tower. Sometimes Sprouse wondered if he should be upset at waking in his windowless bunk every morning, trudging with the others down the dark corridor and sitting in pairs at various points of the conveyer belts that lurched from one side of the workroom to the other. They spent some amount of time, nobody really knew how much, putting together parcels which were cast down a chute by the pairs at the farthest end of the lines. Sprouse and Smith were in the middle of the third belt along, and their job was to place gifts from the basket on the floor beside them into the open boxes. All day every day, reach for the gift, place it in the parcel, reach for the gift, place it in the parcel, a key, a seed packet, a map. Now and then an unknown voice in the back of his thoughts whispered that his former self wouldn't have put up with this, which confused him because he was happy. He got to sit with his friend Smith all day every day, reaching for his own gifts in the mists of nostalgia whilst doing a satisfying day's work.

He was the best at remembering. Occasionally one of the others would hum an old TV theme or recite lines from a show, and the room would chirp along for an hour or two, but Sprouse consistently delivered. He remembered entire episodes of The Dukes of Hazard and whole choruses from pop hits of the 80s. They arrived with no context and left when their work was done, when everyone in the workroom had hummed or chattered their fill over the constant whir of the conveyer belts. "It was sung by a woman," Gibbs might ascertain.

"Didn't she have blonde hair or something?" Harrison might venture. The room would fill with a hundred croaking voices.

"Hey, anyone, wasn't there a show once where one kid wore a helmet so he couldn't see, and the others had to guide him through CGI rooms?" Sprouse sat back, hoping his face didn't blush with pride too much, as the memory snowballed from worker to worker. A more pressing memory threatened to crawl from Sprouse's mind, one of falling further and further down a dark hole until he landed in a place very like this only darker and more threatening, but it made him feel funny so he sang the theme song of the show. Everyone joined in and Sprouse glowed with joy. He reached for the gift and placed it in the parcel, reached for the gift and placed it in the parcel, a bag, a flute, a glittery hat.

Again his wrist exploded with pain and he couldn't stop a small hiss from escaping his lips. His eyes flicked to Smith, whose own remained studiously on her work. To cover his mistake he grasped for a memory, any memory, "what was that movie with..." Sprouse stopped. They all stopped. A name flashed from a sign high up on the wall. "Wh-what does that say?" Sprouse's grip tightened around a brick of Lego and again his tendons twanged like a banjo. Nobody spoke. The conveyer belt surged on and Sprouse's companions hurried to keep up. "I'm not going," he thrust the Lego into the box too hard, tipping it and spilling the tiny red contents. This time he didn't bother suppressing the yelp of pain. Madaki frowned and completed Sprouse's task as well as his own, placing the lid on the parcel and avoiding Sprouse's fearful glare.

"Who...who remembers that song, you know the one, by a brother and sister...or was it cousins?" Sprouse's voice trailed off and he turned from one face to another. All avoided his gaze. "Smith?" Smith frowned but didn't look up. Fury boiled through Sprouse, "Remember it, Smith? It went, dah, dah daaah," He grabbed her shoulder and the agony was instant. He shrieked and doubled over, squeezing his wrist. After several seconds shaking and whimpering, he looked up to see business as usual, as if he'd never been there. It was over. He was damaged goods and had to go upstairs.

He made his way to the door at the back of the workroom and turned the handle shakily. Shadows smothered the staircase behind it and, as he climbed, the door shut leaving him in complete darkness. He gripped the rail and made his way up, pushing down the slimy terror threatening to overflow.

He arrived at a windowless floor with wooden floorboards and a single door at the far end. The air was still and smelled like ancient dust. It was quiet and strangely calming. His footsteps were hollow and his hand steady as he turned the cobwebbed handle. A bright light flooded outwards and Sprouse gasped in shock. Of course, he thought, of course. Everything made sense now. He stepped inside and the slam ricocheted off the walls. Those in the workroom below didn't hear, though, because they were already singing the theme to Thundercats.

ABOUT THE AUTHOR

Madeleine Swann's second novella, 4 Rooms In A Semi-Detached House, was published by StrangeHouse Books, and her first was part of Eraserhead Press' New Bizarro Author Series. Her short stories have appeared in various anthologies and The Wicked Library and Other Stories podcasts.

She makes weird sketches with a friend at DADAkitten. Keep up with her writing at madeleineswann.com and her twitter at https://twitter.com/MadeleineSwann

CPSIA information can be obtained
at www.ICGtesting.com
Printed in the USA
LVOW10s1611220518
578093LV00001B/5/P